"You're despicable!"

He conducted a leisurely appraisal of her stormy features. "We once shared something very special."

"Sex," she flung back at him in utter fury. "Lust," she elaborated accusingly.

"Not two people so in tune with each other that their lovemaking became a beautiful expression of mutual joy?"

Her eyes became luminous, then clouded with bitter pain for a brief second before her lashes swept down to form a protective veil. "It was never like that," she denied shakily.

"No?" His voice was a soft drawl, seductive and infinitely disturbing as his head bent down to hers. "Perhaps I should refresh your memory."

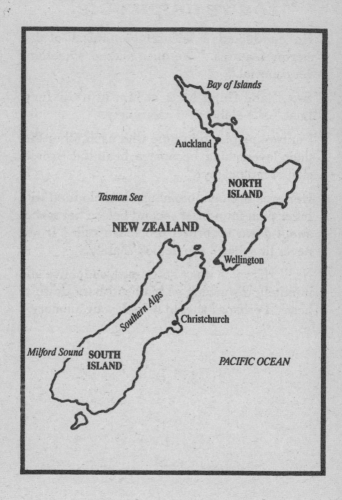

Bay of Islands

Auckland

NORTH ISLAND

Tasman Sea

NEW ZEALAND

Wellington

Southern Alps

Christchurch

Milford Sound **SOUTH ISLAND**

PACIFIC OCEAN

HELEN BIANCHIN

Reluctant Captive

Harlequin Books

TORONTO • NEW YORK • LONDON
AMSTERDAM • PARIS • SYDNEY • HAMBURG
STOCKHOLM • ATHENS • TOKYO • MILAN
MADRID • WARSAW • BUDAPEST • AUCKLAND

ISBN 0-373-11601-2

RELUCTANT CAPTIVE

Copyright © 1992 by Helen Bianchin.

This edition published by arrangement with Harlequin Enterprises B. V.

® and TM are trademarks of the publisher. Trademarks indicated with
® are registered in the United States Patent and Trademark Office, the
Canadian Trade Marks Office and in other countries.

Printed in U.S.A.

CHAPTER ONE

THE far north Queensland town seemed bathed in peaceful tranquillity, Kate mused as she urged the aged and decidedly battered sedan on to the tree-lined street.

During the past few years Port Douglas had gained the reputation of being a first-class tourist resort with the building of a modern hotel, expensive condominiums and a golf-course.

Exotic, expensive, the resort was in stark contrast to its surrounding terrain, and regarded by the locals as a developer's dream several years ahead of its time.

Turning right at the junction linking Mossman to Cairns, Kate drove several kilometres before taking a dirt track leading towards an old wooden cottage nestling close to acres of tall gently waving sugar-cane.

The weathered boards were bare of paint, the iron roof showing visible signs of rust, but the inside was bright and clean, and, most important of all, the rent was cheap.

Three years ago it had been a haven to which she'd escaped from a far distant southern city filled with painful memories. A place that was as removed from her former lifestyle as chalk from cheese.

Now she was locally accepted, bartering organic vegetables grown in a large plot beside the house for fresh farm eggs, carefully nurtured flowers exchanged for fresh fruit. Even the rent was subsidised in exchange for meals she prepared for the elderly widowed farm owner, together with household chores in the main modern home situated a few hundred metres distant.

Kate eased the sedan to a gentle halt beneath the car port, then retrieved her purchases from the rear seat.

The insistent peal of the telephone greeted her as she moved indoors, and she hurried to answer its summons.

'Kate?'

The thick, heavily accented male voice of her landlord and benefactor sounded loud in her ear, and she smiled as she acknowledged his greeting.

'Antonio. I'm preparing your favourite *gnocchi* tonight. With veal *parmigiana* to follow.'

He gave a faint chuckle of appreciation. '*Bene, grazie.*' There was a slight pause. 'Tonight you and Rebecca will join me, yes?'

'For a little while,' she agreed. 'Rebecca has homework, and I have sewing to do for tomorrow.'

'Always work, Kate,' he chided quietly. 'It is good to work, but too much...' He trailed off into eloquent silence, and she could visualise the slight shrug of his shoulders. 'You are young, and your sister, she is——'

'My responsibility, Antonio,' she broke in firmly. 'What shall I make for dessert?' It was a determined bid to change the subject, and she heard the elderly farmer's prodigious sigh in deference to her refusal to further the discussion. 'Brandied pears?' she pursued lightly. 'Or fresh fruit and cream?'

An hour later the preparations were complete, the washing folded and put away, and after a light lunch she entered the spare bedroom to spend essential time at the sewing-machine.

A gifted seamstress, she could turn her hand to almost anything—and did, she mused silently. From craft work to clothes, handknitting to crochet. Most of her wares were sold on consignment to two specialised shops—one of which was in Mossman, the other in Port Douglas. The income was reasonably stable, and sufficient to fund Rebecca's schooling with a little left over for necessities.

As the machine whirred, her thoughts began to dwell on her young sister, and a muttered curse fell from her lips as the needle broke and she had to replace it with another.

At fifteen, Rebecca was becoming increasingly difficult to handle. Normally a sweet-natured even-tempered girl, she'd recently undergone a character change that frequently taxed Kate's patience to its limit. Rebecca's behaviour of late had been more than just normal teenage rebellion, and her grades in school had dropped alarmingly, causing two of her teachers to express concern.

At four o'clock Kate switched off the machine, neatly stacked her work to one side, then entered the kitchen.

A short while later the silence was broken by the familiar sound of the school bus as its creaking brakes brought it to a lumbering halt at the edge of the main road, then the engine groaned laboriously through several gear changes as it gathered speed before disappearing out of sight and sound.

Within minutes the front door opened, then banged shut with an unnecessary force that made Kate wince in sympathy for its well-worn frame. Seconds later she consciously drew in a deep breath and held it as a heavy schoolbag hit the floorboards.

An outward sign that offered little hope of breezy conversation or a smile, Kate acknowledged silently as she called out, 'Hi. I'm in the kitchen.'

'Where else would you be?' came the rather bitter response, and Kate momentarily shut her eyes, then opened them and mentally counted to ten before turning round to greet her sister.

Oh, lord, she sighed, viewing the sulky look of discontent marring Rebecca's attractive features. What now? 'How was your day?' she queried lightly.

'Who cares?'

Kate watched as the young girl extracted a glass then crossed to the refrigerator. It was useless to say *she* cared, and any platitudes would be superfluous.

'Gallagher wants to see you. At ten in his office, Monday.'

The summons could mean only one thing, coming after two recent warnings that any further misdemeanours would not be tolerated.

'At least I'll be out of that rotten place,' Rebecca denounced in a rush of anger. 'It's the pits.'

'That *place*,' Kate said in carefully measured tones, 'provides you with a necessary education.'

'I don't need an education.'

'You do if you want to be employed.'

'Stuff it, Kate,' came the vehement condemnation. 'I don't need a sanctimonious lecture!' The glass banged down on to the table with such force that it was a wonder it didn't shatter. 'Anyway, if Gallagher expels me I'll hitch down to Sydney,' she announced defiantly. 'I'll get a job and a flat. At least life will be exciting for a change.'

'That kind of *excitement* can wait until you've completed all your grades, and passed,' Kate re-iterated firmly, meeting her sister's belligerent glare.

'You can't stop me.'

Oh, *hell*. Why did each new day have to result in yet another battle? 'You can't believe I'll let you go?' Calm, rational, when she felt the need to lose her temper. Maybe that was her mistake, she brooded in despair. Yet somehow she couldn't imagine Rebecca responding to anger, raised voices, or any type of physical punishment.

'I'm not completely stupid. I can look after myself!'

Don't answer that, an inner voice bade her. Any further provocation will achieve absolutely nothing. There was a heavy silence that seemed to last several long seconds.

'Dammit, you're my sister, not my *mother*!' Rebecca burst out.

'Have *you* thought of the worst scenario your idea of an escape from reality could provide?' Kate responded with quiet vehemence. 'Forget hitching, for a start. The chance of finding a sympathetic driver who won't demand sex at the end of the ride is very slim. These days, no references mean no chance of finding decent employment, being on the dole and living in a poky bed-sitting-room you have to pay a small fortune for to be close to transport and the city. Not enough money for food, let alone going out, and you can forget about clothes. What then? Eviction, because you can't pay the rent?' Her eyes sparked with the depth of her emotions. 'At fifteen, you're neither streetwise nor smart enough to live by your wits. But you'll soon have to be, if you want to survive,' she warned without necessary elaboration, aware by the rise of colour in her sister's cheeks that Rebecca understood precisely what she meant. 'Is that really what you want?'

Rebecca's eyes filled with tears of angry resentment. 'I know I don't want to be stuck in a backwater town with no chance of *living*!' She lifted an angry hand and scrubbed the tears from her cheeks. 'I want——'

'Bright lights, big city,' Kate supplied with more than a touch of cynicism.

'*Yes*! What's so wrong with that?'

'Nothing,' she said wearily. 'Except—go prepared, with the necessary qualifications needed to gain a good salary, which will provide the money needed for a nice flat in a fashionable suburb.' She felt tired, drained emotionally and physically from their continual quarrels. 'Believe me, anything less is a recipe for disaster.'

'You think I'm three years ahead of myself, don't you?'

Kate summoned a faintly rueful smile. 'Will you shoot me down in flames if I say *yes*?'

'*Damn*!' the younger girl cursed. 'I want so much, and I want it *now*. Sydney is my home town. I loved it when we lived there. Why did we have to *leave*?'

Kate felt her eyes cloud with remembered pain, and for a few seconds she was silent before venturing quietly, 'You were too young to understand,' she began slowly.

'*Why* won't you ever discuss it?' Rebecca burst out in condemnation.

'What good will it do to rehash the sordid details of my disastrous marriage?' Kate countered.

'I *liked* Nicolas,' the younger girl flared, and Kate drew in a deep, steadying breath.

'You saw him through the eyes of an eleven-year-old child,' she reminded her with a touch of cynicism. Whereas *I* struck a bargain with *el diablo* himself, and couldn't live with the consequences, she added silently.

'Life isn't *fair*!'

No, it's not, Kate echoed silently. Unfortunately that's the first in a series of hard lessons you have to learn. As I did.

'Antonio would like us to join him for dinner tonight,' she declared in an attempt to change the subject.

'I'd rather stay home.'

As much as she wanted to insist, maybe capitulation was a wiser alternative. 'I won't be late. I have some sewing to finish,' she said in a carefully neutral voice, and saw the flash of bitterness evident in the younger girl's features.

'You're *always* sewing or doing something!' Her eyes sparked with angry censure. 'I don't want to end up like you, buried in a small country town and old before my time. Can't you *see* what you've become, for heaven's sake?'

Kate felt the colour drain from her face, and she clenched her hands until the knuckles shone white. 'However badly done by you imagine yourself to be, I won't allow you to treat me as your personal punching bag. I think it would be best if you went to your room for a while until you cool down.'

'I'll ring Sandra and spend the night at her place.' Truculence vied with anger and sheer, impotent frustration. 'That way I'll be completely out of your hair for twenty-four hours. I might even stay over the entire weekend and go to school with her Monday morning.'

The instinct to say no was overridden by a desire for peace—if only overnight. There was too much resentment buried in Rebecca's psyche for any passive resolution of this current crisis. Tomorrow she'd undoubtedly regret taking the easy way out. 'If Sandra's mother says it's OK,' she qualified.

Rebecca crossed at once to the phone and dialled the necessary digits, spoke to her friend, then silently handed the receiver to Kate with what could only be described as a smirk of satisfaction.

Five minutes later Kate replaced the receiver with a feeling of guilty relief at the thought of respite. 'Sandra's mother has invited you to dinner. She'll drive by and pick you up in half an hour.'

'Great. I'll see you Monday.'

At five-thirty Kate quickly showered, then she slipped into fresh clothes before tending to her hair. A quick encompassing glance at her mirrored image reflected her petite small-boned frame and slim curves. With her long ash-blonde hair twisted into a single thick braid that reached beneath her shoulder-blades, she looked much younger than her twenty-five years.

It was almost six when Kate placed containers into a large wicker basket, then locked the door behind her prior to walking the short distance to the main house.

Her bright smile on greeting Antonio didn't fool him in the least, and his soul-searching scrutiny of her pale features, the silent sympathy evident, made her feel defenceless and strangely vulnerable.

Kate merely picked at the small serving she apportioned herself, and attempted an interest in Antonio's reminiscences. A gifted raconteur, he would have made an excellent father and grandfather, but, as he'd shrugged with philosophic fatalism, the good *Dio* had opted not to bless his beloved Carla with children.

'So, what will you do this weekend with no Rebecca to stir up the waves, hm?'

A faint smile of amusement lightened her features, and he leaned well back in his chair as she poured his coffee.

'Ah, at last. A little glimpse of my good-natured Kate.'

'Not so good-natured,' she dismissed wryly.

'There should be a man by your side,' Antonio said gently. 'Someone strong, who would remove the weight from your small shoulders.'

There was once. Except we married for all the wrong reasons, and I could never justify any one of them as being right. Besides, I was too young, too naïve, and he was a thousand light-years ahead of me in every way.

Aloud, she ventured, 'I don't think I need any added complications right now.'

'Eventually Rebecca will grow up and leave home. The child is an exotic butterfly. What will you do then, my beautiful Kate?'

'Lead a peaceful existence?' she countered musingly, and saw the slow negating movement of his head.

'Alone?'

'Is solitude such a bad thing?'

A smile creased his broad, lined Latin features. 'For an old man like me? No. For someone as young and beautiful as you, it is a waste.'

'Not if I'm content.'

A faint shadow dulled his eyes, then he pushed forward his cup. 'Pour me another coffee, *cara*. After, I will walk you home.'

Kate knew better than to argue with him, especially in winter when it was dark, and twenty minutes later she watched him traverse the well-worn track back to the main house.

The weekend passed all too swiftly as Kate attended to a number of chores. There was no phone call from Rebecca, but she hadn't expected one, and Monday morning she rose with a sinking heart at the prospect of her appointment with the school's headmaster.

Kate dressed with care, taking more time with her hair and make-up than usual in the hope that it would boost her confidence sufficient to deal with a world-weary man whose patience had long worn thin over the years with having to cope with numerous teenage recalcitrants and their long-suffering parents.

'I cannot permit Rebecca's disruptive behaviour to continue in class.'

Kate heard the words and mentally braced herself to plead her sister's case—even beg if she had to. 'Mr Gallagher, surely if I give you my assurance it won't happen again you could veer towards leniency?'

'I've already done that—twice. The last occasion incurred a very real warning that, if there was cause for a further summons to my office, I would have little option but to consider expulsion.' He picked up his pen and began twisting it abstractedly between the fingers of one hand. 'A fact Rebecca has obviously taken for granted, since she hasn't arrived in class today.'

'Not arrived?' Kate queried with genuine perplexity. 'But of course she has. She spent the weekend with Sandra Patrullo. They came to school together this morning.'

'I'm afraid Rebecca did not. I can check on Sandra, if you'll excuse me for the few minutes it will take to speak with her teacher?' He leaned forward, activated a call through to the appropriate classroom, spoke briefly into the receiver, listened, then bade Sandra be sent at once to his office.

Kate began to feel a sense of rising panic that mounted considerably when Sandra entered the office looking apprehensive.

It transpired that Sandra's brother had taken the girls into Mossman to the cinema, where Sandra had fallen ill and her brother had driven her home, returning for Rebecca, who had opted not to stay over as arranged. On the way back his car had developed a puncture, and when a close friend had stopped to give assistance, the friend had offered to drive Rebecca back to the cottage.

Kate tried to remain calm as fear began an all-consuming grip on her sanity. 'Rebecca hasn't been home,' she declared, clarifying the fact as she turned towards the headmaster. 'We have to contact the police.'

'Before we do that I think you should speak to Sandra's brother.'

What followed became a nightmare, as two further phone calls revealed Rebecca's deliberate deception in begging a lift to Cairns with the intention of going standby on the early morning flight to Sydney.

Kate heard the words with a sinking heart, and took an even tighter grip of the receiver. 'Did Rebecca tell you what her plans were when she reached Sydney?'

'She assured me she had a place to stay and the prospect of a job.' The young man's conscience appeared to get the better of him. 'I wouldn't have lent her money, or let her go, otherwise.'

Kate longed to fling that he should have had more sense than to aid and abet a totally irresponsible fifteen-year-old girl whose single-minded wilfulness was not only reprehensible but also liable, unless she was extremely fortunate, to land her in a whole heap of trouble.

Instead, she drew in a deep, steadying breath, thanked him, then replaced the receiver. Turning towards the headmaster, she schooled her voice into a semblance of calm as she relayed the conversation.

Despite extensive questioning, Sandra appeared genuinely unable to confirm that Rebecca's action hadn't been premeditated, nor could she shed any light on where Rebecca intended staying, or with whom. The only confirmation she could give was Rebecca's determination to return to Sydney.

'Honestly, Kate,' the young girl assured earnestly, 'it's all she ever talked about.'

'Is there no one you can contact in Sydney who might be aware of her whereabouts?'

Kate momentarily closed her eyes at the headmaster's words, then slowly opened them again. 'No. At least, no one I can immediately think of.'

Liar, an inner voice taunted. There is one person. Someone whose wealth and power will ensure no stone remains unturned.

If the police enquiry fails I'll ring Nicolas, she assured herself shakily, knowing with a kind of detached fatalism that she would have no other choice. Her fear for her sister would override any previous resolve.

Slowly she rose to her feet, thanked the headmaster and Sandra, for their concern, and promised she would be in touch as soon as she had any news.

Somehow she managed to walk to her car, and it was a minor miracle that she managed the short drive to the police station without incident.

There, a kind, fatherly man took details, asked relevant questions, completed necessary paperwork, and advised her to go home and wait by the phone. He would ring, he assured, the instant he had any news.

Kate drove home in a daze, alternating between fear and anger until both merged as one, feeding her imagination with differing horrific scenarios until she felt physically ill.

On reaching the cottage, she brought the car to a standstill, and for a few infinitesimal seconds she sat slumped behind the wheel, unwilling to emerge and face being alone.

A strange prickling sensation began at her nape, then rapidly spread over the surface of her skin, almost as if in recognition of some elusive premonition.

Crazy, she dismissed instantly as she opened the car door and slid to her feet.

There was work to do, she decided dully as she crossed round to the front of the house and trod the worn steps on to the veranda. Perhaps that was the panacea she needed—to immerse herself in sewing to the extent that she was no longer conscious of the agonising *waiting* period until the police could provide some answers.

Without thought she simply unlocked the cottage and went straight through to the spare room to switch on the sewing-machine, aware within minutes that sheer automation had taken over as her fingers instinctively guided fabric beneath the needle.

No matter how hard she tried, it was impossible to dispel the feeling of anxiety as she agonised over Rebecca's whereabouts, and time dragged, with each ensuing minute seeming like at least ten.

The sound of tyres crunching to a halt outside the cottage alerted her attention, and she flew towards the rear veranda with such speed that the driver had scarcely sufficient time to switch off the ignition, let alone alight from the car.

Heart in mouth, Kate viewed the vehicle with puzzled perplexity. She'd expected a phone call, not a personal visit from the police.

Yet this wasn't an official car, nor was the man who stepped out from behind the wheel a representative of any law-enforcement team.

His strongly etched features were only too familiar, his tall, impressive stature just as arresting as when she'd last seen him.

Shock momentarily froze her into immobility, robbing her pale skin of any semblance of colour, and a wave of dizziness assailed her, sweeping through her body with debilitating swiftness. For a moment she thought she might actually faint, and she clutched hold of the door for support.

Nicolas Carvalho. Son of a Spanish immigrant who had gone from rags to riches by speculating in property development, he now headed a veritable empire.

He was also the man from whom she'd fled almost three years previously, and someone she deemed to be part of her past.

CHAPTER TWO

'HELLO, Kate.'

Visions didn't possess voices. At least, not to her knowledge, and *not*, she accepted grimly, with quite the cynical inflexion Nicolas Carvalho afforded on occasion. He could, she remembered all too vividly, reduce the most strong-minded person to a quivering wreck without any seeming effort at all.

Three years had wrought very little change, she noted warily.

If it was possible, he appeared even more riveting than before, his intensely masculine frame emanating an animalistic power and innate sexuality that was both potent and lethal. A man from whom any sensible woman would run *fast*, and as far as her virtue demanded.

His broad facial bone-structure was well-chiselled, although the grooves slashing each cheek seemed a fraction deeper than she remembered, and unless she was mistaken there were a few strands of grey among his black well-groomed hair.

The dark brown eyes were just as intense, she observed, and had lost none of their ability to sear the soul.

A faint shiver feathered her soft body hairs in vivid memory of the manner in which he was able to elicit the most craven response. Almost as if he held licence to a woman's innermost need.

In the business arena he was a feared adversary, his strength of purpose chilling and deadly. Yet his integrity was beyond reproach, his generosity to charity legendary. However, no one with an ounce of sense would dare cross him—in revenge, he was known to be killingly swift.

'Have you finished?'

His deep drawl sent an icy chill feathering across the surface of her skin, and her startled gaze locked with his for a brief second before his eyes swept her features in a raking, all-encompassing appraisal that brought a rush of colour to her cheeks.

'I can't imagine what you're doing here.' Her eyes held hidden anger, their sapphire-blue depths gleaming with the extent of her emotions, and her chin took on a defensive tilt as she held his gaze.

She was suddenly conscious of her attire, the neat pale blue cotton trousers topped with a dusky pink handknitted short-sleeved jumper, and her long, naturally curly ash-blonde hair lay in a thick, casually contrived coil at her nape.

No longer standing at the foot of the steps, he had silently ascended to the veranda, and she was tempted to move back a few steps to lessen the feeling of intimidation his height provided.

'This isn't a good time to visit,' Kate managed in an oddly taut voice, and her hand lifted in a defensive gesture as she tucked a stray tendril of hair behind her ear.

'Irrespective of how hateful you find my presence,' Nicolas told her wryly, 'I think you'll welcome the news that Rebecca is safe.'

'Rebecca has contacted *you*?' she queried in shocked disbelief, unable in the few following seconds to assimilate anything.

'Shall we go indoors?'

There was a certain futility in conducting an argument on the doorstep, and she preceded him into the kitchen, anger mounting with every passing second.

'Don't you realise I've been almost out of my mind with worry? Dammit,' she threw in fully fledged fury, 'she's been gone three *days*!'

'A fact you only discovered just over an hour ago,' he reminded in a hateful drawl. 'Is this not so?'

Without warning, her hand flew in a swift arc towards his face, and she cried out as he intercepted it and caught her wrist in a painful grip.

'Don't you *dare* insinuate I'm wanting in any way with regard to Rebecca's welfare! Let me go, damn you!' Her eyes were stormy with angry, frustrated tears, and she wrenched her wrist free—only because he allowed it. The delicate collection of bones felt utterly bruised, the skin protecting them white and incredibly tender, and she mechanically massaged the affected wrist in an attempt to ease the pain.

'I have to phone the police, the head-master——'

'I've already taken care of it,' Nicolas informed her in a ruthless voice, and a chill shiver feathered its way down the length of her spine.

It was impossible to dispel a feeling of resentment at his high-handedness, as well as a compelling desire to discover why he had flown several thousand kilometres when he could easily have picked up the phone.

'Where is she?' Kate demanded, and his appraisal was swift and analytical as it raked her petite form.

'Sydney.'

'You didn't bring her back with you?' A pulse started hammering in her throat, and it took all her courage to restrain her temper.

'I'll let Rebecca give you a detailed account of her so-called adventure,' Nicolas revealed in a voice that would have daunted even the most unwary opponent. 'The condensed version is that she arrived in Sydney with twenty dollars in her pocket,' he continued drily, and his rough-chiselled features assumed a hard implacability. 'The contact she imagined she could rely on proved unavailable, and with nowhere to stay she booked herself into a hotel, ordering room service for meals. When approached by management about the length of her stay and the method of settling her account, she prevaricated and attempted to leave without paying. She was apprehended,' he elaborated, watching the expressive play of emotions evident in her pale features. 'The police were called, and she was charged. Faced with the reality of having committed a crime, she at least had the presence of mind to contact me.'

'Rebecca is in custody?' The thought made her physically ill, and her eyes were impossibly wide with distress.

'I had a lawyer arrange for her to be released into my care on my personal undertaking that she would appear in court tomorrow. At the moment she's safely ensconced with my mother, and under strict instructions not to move one inch outside the grounds.'

Dear heaven, this was like a living nightmare! Where was she going to find the money to pay for legal representation? What was more, she'd have to go down to Sydney, for there could be no question of allowing Nicolas to assume responsibility.

'Sit down,' Nicolas instructed, and, extending an arm, he pulled out a chair. 'You look positively wraith-like.'

He towered head and shoulders above her, making her feel inadequate and singularly ineffectual. If she sat down it would only succeed in diminishing her self-confidence, and that would never do.

Animosity rose to the fore, and was reflected in the dark glare she spared him. 'I'd rather stand.'

'Still the same Kate, I see,' he said with musing cynicism, and she took a deep steadying breath in a concentrated effort not to digress into sheer unadulterated anger.

'And *you*,' she intoned heatedly, 'are just as impossibly overbearing as ever!'

'The main issue is Rebecca, surely?' His eyes glittered with ruthless disregard. 'Despite our——' he paused imperceptibly '—differences, you can't deny she seems caught in a trap of her own teenage rebellion. The question,' he continued with deceptive softness, 'is what we're going to do about it.'

'There is no *we*,' she reiterated in angry rejection. 'Rebecca is *my* responsibility!'

'I'm not disputing it,' Nicolas declared hardily. 'However, at the present moment she's compelled to remain under my care until the current matter is resolved. I instructed my lawyer to offer the hotel manager a commensurate sum in the hope of having the charges dropped.' His eyes hardened measurably. 'It seems, though, that the manager is determined to make an example of Rebecca's actions and have his day in court.'

Kate looked at him in horror. 'It could take weeks——'

'Indeed,' he agreed, subjecting her to a raking scrutiny. 'If it helps, Rebecca appears suitably chagrined.'

Faced with Nicolas's analytical logic, only the most hardened sophisticate would choose to challenge him. A mere child stood no chance whatsoever.

How could she stay in Sydney for more than a few days? Kate agonised, mentally reviewing her meagre savings.

'Whatever else is a consideration, *money*—or your lack of it—isn't an issue.' The directive was hard and inflexible. 'Nor,' he added with chilling softness, 'where or with whom you'll stay.'

'I refuse to be beholden to you in any way!'

For one crazy moment she thought he was about to lose his temper. 'Go and pack, Kate,' he said with dangerous silkiness.

Her head tilted, and there was the light of battle in her eyes. 'I have to prepare Antonio's dinner.'

'I've already spoken with him.'

Shock momentarily robbed her of speech. 'You *know* Antonio?'

His smile was a mere facsimile, and failed to reach the darkness of his eyes. 'Antonio is an old friend of my father's. They both emigrated from their own country within months of each other to work the cane-fields. Antonio stayed in the far north, married, and went on to buy his own farm. My father preferred the acquisition of a higher education, and the faster pace of city life.'

Twin flags of colour highlighted the sharp bones of her cheeks. 'You've known all along that I lived *here*?'

She saw his eyes darken fractionally, then assume an inscrutability that was impossible to penetrate. 'I was aware of your precise whereabouts within twenty-four hours of when you left me.'

A number of conflicting emotions vied for supremacy as she fought for control and lost. 'You hired a detective, and had someone watch me, *follow* me?' she queried in scandalised disbelief.

'You think *chance* was responsible for this cottage being so conveniently available at such a cheap rental?'

'Next you'll tell me Antonio merely acted a part,' she said with angry bitterness, her illusions almost totally shattered. Resentment flared briefly as she met his steady gaze and the cool, assessing quality apparent there.

'Antonio repaid a favour,' Nicolas informed without any scruple. 'Then became enchanted by your kindness and unstinting generosity towards him.' He pulled back the cuff of his jacket as he spared his watch a glance. 'There's a chartered jet waiting in Cairns. The pilot has instructions to be ready at two.' His eyes bored hers, darkly intense for a brief second. 'I suggest you begin packing.'

She wanted to rage against fate, against *him*, and more than anything she wanted to ruffle his imperturbable composure. The light of battle lent her eyes a dangerous sparkle.

'Don't waste time, Kate.'

He sounded amused, damn him. Almost as if he could read her thoughts, and that rankled almost beyond her endurance. 'You have no right to walk in here and issue orders!'

For a long moment he just looked at her, then he relayed silkily, 'I leave here in ten minutes. Choose whether you want to pack, or have me do it for you.'

There could be no contest, and without a further word she turned and walked into her bedroom, retrieved a suitcase, and began tossing in articles of clothing without any rational thought.

Opting for a change of attire, she donned a pair of tailored cotton trousers and a white and beige striped long-sleeved shirt, then slung a patterned jumper in varying shades of brown across her shoulders and fastened the sleeves together in a casual knot beneath her throat.

A quick collection of toiletries from the bathroom, and she was ready. With a few minutes to spare, she perceived as she cast her watch a quick glance.

'I'll have to make a few phone calls,' Kate informed him as Nicolas took the case from her hand.

'Do it in the car, from my cellular unit.' His dark piercing gaze made a mockery of anything further she might offer, and she closed her lips tightly against the stream of words she longed to heap on his diabolical head.

The mobile phone was a blessing, and she placed a few essential calls before lapsing into silence as she concentrated her gaze on the passing scenery.

Dimensional rays of sunlight fingered the dark mountain foliage, accentuating the range's rolling contours as they neared the outskirts of Cairns. In contrast were acres of towering cane, interspersed with several paddocks of fresh-ploughed earth, while vibrant multicoloured hibiscus and beautiful spreading boughs of purple jacaranda graced the grounds surrounding a number of farmhouses.

At the airport a sleek private jet stood waiting for them, and Kate walked out on to the tarmac at Nicolas's side, boarded, then took the seat he indicated.

Five minutes later they were airborne, and she simply caught up a magazine and pretended interest in an article on the conception and birth of a rare breed of tropical fish.

Nicolas ordered lunch from the attendant hostess, and when Kate shook her head, he overruled her in a voice that verged on condescension.

'I won't be patronised,' she threw in a resentful undertone. 'Besides, I'm not hungry,' she added, and bore his dark enigmatic gaze with contrived steadiness.

'Eat, Kate,' he insisted imperturbably. 'You look so impossibly fragile that it scares me.'

'I refuse to believe anything scares you,' she retorted, all too aware of his close proximity and the devastating effect he had on her equilibrium. 'Entire corporations tremble at the mere mention of your name, and women fall over themselves in a bid for your attention.'

'You were an exception,' he drawled, his gaze direct and analytical.

'Because I failed to be impressed by your millions, or to join half the female population of Sydney who viewed the dynamic Nicolas Carvalho as the ultimate sex symbol?'

'Yet you married me,' Nicolas reminded, and her chin lifted fractionally as she dredged into her reserves of strength.

'It seemed like a good idea at the time.' Her voice was remarkably even, belying the emotional havoc deep within.

'"An honest arrangement", I distinctly remember you calling our liaison. Based on necessity, and mutually convenient,' he declared with thinly veiled mockery, and she held his gaze without any difficulty at all.

Her necessity, his convenience. Arranged and presented by *his* mother as a solution to ease *her* mother's anxiety. The fact that the women had been close friends since childhood, and had maintained that friendship long after each had married and raised children, said something for the shared bond. Especially as Esther Carvalho's fortune accelerated beyond her wildest dreams via her husband's entrepreneurial skills, while Suzanne Sloane suffered a reversal as she was thrust into widowhood at an early age, only to slip from this world after chemotherapy failed to halt the ravages of cancer.

Suzanne, however, survived long enough to see her eldest daughter married in what was described as the social wedding of the year. She died at peace, content in the knowledge that Kate and Rebecca were adequately cared for by the omnipotent Carvalho family.

What her mother failed to foresee, Kate reflected bitterly, was that society gossip became responsible for a plethora of damaging facts. The most hurtful being that Nicolas Carvalho viewed his marriage to Kate as a suitable smokescreen for his affair with a married socialite. Nor did it help to discover that Esther Carvalho had forked out a veritable fortune in medical bills for the all but destitute Suzanne.

Instead of accepting her fate, Kate soon began to find the situation increasingly impossible. Arguments with Nicolas digressed into frequent battles, until, disillusioned and unwilling to continue living a lie, she made a conscious decision to leave.

A few days after an elaborate party to celebrate their first wedding anniversary, Kate had simply packed a bag, propped a written note within plain sight for Nicolas, collected Rebecca from school and bundled them both on a plane to Brisbane. There she began covering her tracks, establishing an elaborate network that involved a *poste restante* address, despatched a carefully written letter to Esther Carvalho, and elicited the help of a very dear friend to collect and forward all future mail. Then, together with Rebecca, she boarded an evening flight to Cairns in an effort to seek a fresh start far away from everything and everyone she'd ever known.

The contact with Esther Carvalho was maintained via letters regularly mailed to the Brisbane address, whereupon Kate's friend would extract the envelope and send it on to Sydney. Esther's letters to Kate were treated in a similar fashion. However, the account Esther opened for her daughter-in-law with a Brisbane bank remained untouched.

An elaborate but worthless charade, Kate mused in silent frustration as she viewed the soft cotton-wool clouds beyond the jet's window. The Carvalho family simply extended its powerful contacts, and had been informed of her every move.

Now she was being forcibly returned to their bosom, a victim this time of her sister. But not for long, a tiny voice prompted with grim determination. A few weeks was all it would take. Then she'd bring a hopefully chastened Rebecca home, and attempt to instil a modicum of common sense into her mutinous head.

Ignoring the lunch tray, she closed her eyes as the enormity of the last few hours caught up with her, together with a host of possible consequences that persistently presented themselves.

'Refusing to eat won't achieve anything,' Nicolas directed with pitiless disregard. 'Have a small glass of wine. It will boost your appetite.'

'If I refuse, will you treat me like the child you think I am, and forcibly make me drink?'

'Am I treating you like a child?'

He hadn't changed, she perceived wearily. He was still the same Nicolas, adroitly answering a question with another and turning the tables on an unsuspecting quarry. Except she was no longer unsuspecting, or naïve.

'You always have,' Kate told him with swift anger. 'I used to think it had everything to do with my stature.'

'Five feet two inches of volatile femininity,' he conceded musingly, 'who now purports to be a mature, thinking young woman.'

Her eyes blazed a brilliant blue. '*Yes*.' To prove it, she picked at the salad, ate the fruit compote, and had two glasses of mineral water.

Steadily the aeronautical miles between Cairns and Sydney diminished, and as they drew closer to their destination Kate began to experience the feeling of unease.

During the past three years she'd become accustomed to the laid-back casual north Queensland lifestyle, far removed from the huge, bustling metropolis of Sydney. Within the space of a few hours she'd have to face Esther and Rafael Carvalho, and attempt to deal with Rebecca.

Fifteen minutes out of Sydney they ran into a storm, which lashed the plane with wind-driven rain, proving on disembarkation to be chillingly cold and penetrated right through to her bones.

An omen? Kate pondered as she sank into the rear of Nicolas's turbo-charged Bentley, chauffeur-driven by Sebastian Evans, who, together with his wife Mary, took care of Nicolas's house and grounds.

The heated warmth of the car's interior took the sting from the outdoor temperatures, and soon dried the few droplets of rain from her clothes.

'Relax,' Nicolas drawled, and she cast him a long considering look, holding his steady gaze with equanimity.

'I feel as if I'm about to enter the lion's den,' she said with a slight edge of cynicism that brought a faint lift of his eyebrow.

'My mother adores you, as does my father,' he responded with an indolence that didn't fool her in the slightest. 'Rebecca, I'm sure, will be only too eager to seek atonement.'

'And you, Nicolas,' she pursued relentlessly. 'What part do you play in all of this?'

'The role of mediator?'

'I know you too well to believe that's your sole motive.'

His expression was impossible to define, and for some unknown reason she felt all her fine body hairs stand up in a involuntary gesture of self-defence.

'Your imagination is working overtime,' he denied in a voice that was dangerously silky, and succeeded in sending shivers of apprehension slithering down the length of her spine.

It was crazy to imagine that the man seated beside her posed a threat. Yet she felt as if she was treading eggshells, frighteningly aware that one false step would unleash a multitude of emotions, none of which she was suitably equipped to deal with.

Three years apart hadn't dimmed the intense effect he had on her equilibrium. The memory of that powerful body, naked, entwined with her own, and held in the thrall of uninhibited passion, was startlingly clear. So clear that she was unable to suppress a visible shiver as it shook her slender frame.

'Cold?'

His voice belied its softness, and she ignored the element of taunting cynicism apparent, turning away from him as she focused her attention on the scenery beyond the darkened window.

Traffic was heavy on the main arterial roads, frequently slowing to a complete standstill. Every computer-controlled intersection seemed to be bringing her inexorably closer to a situation from which she instinctively wanted to withdraw.

Deep within the far reaches of her mind was a little voice that kept taunting, He has you on his territory, and already he's pulling the strings.

It was after six when the car swept through ornate cast-iron gates into a long curving driveway leading to Esther and Rafael Carvalho's elegant Spanish-styled mansion positioned high on a hill in the fashionable suburb of Vaucluse.

Security measures were at a premium, and Kate knew that sensor pads and laser beams linked up to a highly sophisticated electronic surveillance alarm system inside the house ensured that no one, not even an animal, could enter the gates or scale the walls undetected.

A blaze of light outlined the large whitewashed stone villa, its wide pillared portico and double entrance doors exuding a welcome to invited guests as the car drew to a smooth halt.

Almost at once the doors swung open to reveal Nicolas's parents in their aperture for an instant before they descended the few steps to the terracotta-tiled forecourt.

There was a terrible sense of *déjà vu* as Kate stepped out of the Bentley and into the outstretched arms of Esther Carvalho.

'My dear, how simply wonderful to see you again.'

The affection was genuine, as was the embrace, and Kate felt her eyes sting with suppressed emotion as she returned the warm hug Nicolas's mother afforded her before being passed into Rafael's bear-like embrace.

'Come indoors,' Rafael bade as soon as he released her. 'It is cold, and we cannot have you becoming ill.'

His dark eyes conducted a swift sweeping appraisal of her slim form, and she sensed a hint of his disapproval for her diminished curves.

The foyer was exactly as Kate remembered, and she walked at Rafael's side as he led her into the large luxuriously appointed lounge.

A slight figure rose from one of the chairs and hurled herself into Kate's arms, almost sobbing with a mixture of apprehension and relief.

'Oh, Kate, I'm sorry,' Rebecca began with genuine remorse. 'I didn't mean for it to turn out like this.'

Kate hugged Rebecca close, then gently disentangled her arms. 'I know.' There were a number of things she wanted to say, but now was not the time for remonstrance. Later, when they were alone, she could persuade Rebecca to fill in all the gaps and take her to task.

'What will you have to drink, Kate?'

Normally she rarely indulged in anything alcoholic, but she needed something to dull the sharp edges the past nine hours had provided.

Turning towards Rafael, she offered a faint smile. 'White wine, not too sweet.'

Her fingers shook slightly as she accepted the slim crystal flute from his hand, and she glimpsed the faint narrowing of his eyes and their resultant concern.

'You have nothing to fear,' he reassured quietly. 'Nicolas has everything beneath his control.'

She didn't doubt it for a moment. The only doubt she had was Nicolas's motive. 'I can't begin to thank you.'

'Dinner will be served in fifteen minutes,' Esther declared, her brown eyes warm with kindness as they rested on Kate's expressive features. 'Perhaps you'd like to take the opportunity to freshen up? A shower and change of clothes, if you so choose.'

Kate clutched at the excuse to escape. 'Would you mind?'

'Of course not, my dear. Sophy will have taken your bag to the blue room.'

Scarcely a true description, Kate accorded as she quietly closed the door of the guest room behind her. The magnificent home was a visual attestation to style and elegance, filled with gracious antique furniture, and a uniformity in curtains and soft furnishings. Subtle introduction of colour was incorporated in the sumptuous bedcover, upholstered velvet *chaise-longue* and dressing-table chair.

Nine minutes later she was ready, considerably refreshed after a quick shower, and reasonably confident in a change of clothes. Slender-heeled shoes lent her diminutive stature added inches, and she'd deliberately confined her make-up to lipstick and a touch of eyeshadow.

The carved balustrade of the gently curving staircase was smooth to her touch as she quickly descended to the ground floor, and her steps faltered slightly as she reached the door leading into the lounge.

Don't be silly, she silently admonished. They're only human. Esther and Rafael, Rebecca—*yes*, a tiny voice taunted. But what of Nicolas?

Taking a deep breath, she summoned a smile and re-entered the spacious room, unutterably relieved to discover Rafael and Nicolas seemingly deep in conversation.

Dinner was announced precisely five minutes later, and she walked with Esther and Rebecca into the large formal dining-room, aware that Nicolas and his father followed at a more leisurely pace.

The food was superb, each course a visual attestation to the chef's cordon bleu proficiency. Yet Kate could have been eating sawdust for all the enjoyment she derived as she forked a few selected morsels from her plate.

Even the wine, despite being of excellent vintage, did little to restore her appetite, and she was supremely conscious of Nicolas's veiled scrutiny throughout the meal.

Esther, a supreme hostess, managed with the ease of long practice to bring a sense of normality to the ensuing few hours, and to a casual observer it would appear they were a relaxed group of people who bore each other a strong measure of affection.

Yet beneath the façade of politeness Kate felt on edge and filled with an inexplicable sense of anxiety.

'Shall we adjourn to the lounge for coffee?'

It was almost ten o'clock, and she would have given anything to be able to excuse herself and go to bed. A tension headache had manifested itself, without doubt a result of the day's events, and she longed for solitude and the merciful oblivion sleep would bring.

'I think not, Mama,' Nicolas refused. 'If you'll excuse us, we'll leave.'

We? Surely she and Rebecca were staying *here*? Nicolas couldn't expect her to return like a docile lamb to the home she'd shared with him during their marriage?

Yet one glance at his hard chiselled features was sufficient to ascertain that he had every intention of insisting upon it, should she dare to be so foolish as to resist. It was there in the darkness of his eyes, the firm set of his jaw.

'Of course,' Esther conceded graciously. 'There is the anxiety of tomorrow. Besides, you have much to talk about.' She caught a glimpse of Kate's surprised expression, and briefly took hold of her hand. 'My dear, sleep well. I'll look forward to seeing you again very soon.'

Kate thanked Esther and Rafael for their hospitality, then followed Rebecca into the rear of the Bentley.

Why did she feel as if events were rapidly getting out of hand? Surely everything had already been settled?

Nicolas's residence was a few short blocks distant, situated in an equally prestigious street and sharing a similar view. Spacious and elegant, it was Tudor in design and built of mellow grey stone, the leadlight mullioned windows lending innate charm to a home Kate had adored on sight, its visual perfection enhanced by an abundance of rose gardens set in beautiful sculpted grounds.

Almost on cue, the car slowed, passed through electronically controlled gates, then slowly traversed the gently curved pebbled driveway.

Very little had changed, Kate registered dully as she took in the gardens and the house itself. Bathed in light, it presented a silent welcome she was loath to recognise, let alone admit to, and she experienced a feeling of reluctance as Nicolas alighted and held open her door.

The interior was exactly as she remembered. Soft grey textured carpet provided a perfect foil for the rosewood antique-fashioned furniture. Large rooms acquired a delightful spaciousness with high ceilings offset by exquisite crystal chandeliers. Built on two levels, the ground floor comprised a number of formal rooms used for entertaining, an informal family room and dining-room and a large modern kitchen. There was also a study, which was solely Nicolas's domain. A wide curving staircase led to the master bedroom suite, with its own *en suite* and an adjoining sitting-room, as well as four bed-rooms, each with its own *en suite*.

Kate had the strangest feeling that, if she blinked, the past three years would disappear. Crazy, she chided silently. *Insane.*

'Mary Evans will have retired for the night,' Nicolas intoned smoothly as he moved towards the lounge. 'Would you mind making some coffee, Rebecca?'

A heightened sixth sense seemed hell-bent on bringing all her defences to the fore, and Kate experienced distinct misgivings at her sister's enthusi-astic alacrity to perform Nicolas's request.

'It's been a long, fraught day,' she said wearily, opting to ignore his silent gesture to be seated in one of several elegant cushioned chairs positioned around the large room. 'I'd prefer to forgo coffee, if you don't mind.'

'By all means.' He was standing within touching distance, and she could almost feel the warmth of his body, *sense* the strength emanating from his superbly muscled frame. Exuding sheer animal magnetism, he possessed the power to stir her senses, bringing alive an awareness she found vaguely shocking. 'However, there is something we have to discuss.'

'Can't it wait until morning?'

'No.' The calm, rational refusal held hidden steel, and she lifted her eyes to meet his in a gesture of stormy defiance.

'This had better directly concern Rebecca.'

'Sit down.'

'And have you tower over me like some feudal lord?'

He smiled, a slow, indolent movement of his lips that riveted her attention. Beneath her anger was a terrible fascination to have that mouth close over her own in a need to discover if his kiss still felt the same.

You're *crazy*, an inner voice taunted. He hurt you so badly that you ran away, and you hate him, remember? Hate everything about him.

'Of any of the many names you called me, I fail to recall that particular combination,' he said with soft cynicism. 'Sit down, Kate,' he bade her silkily. 'This could take a while.'

Oh, what was the use? she thought wretchedly as she subsided into the nearest chair. She wasn't in any mood to fight, and past experience had only proved that opposing him was a fruitless exercise.

'Tomorrow my legal representative will request an adjournment, and, with the backlog of cases awaiting trial before the court, he expects it will be several weeks before Rebecca's case is heard. Time that can be used to her advantage, if it can be proved she has settled well in school and is able to produce favourable references from her teachers and the headmistress. Irrefutably advantageous,' he continued deliberately, 'if there is attested proof of a solid family background with two stable guardians.'

Kate heard the words and assimilated them, her nerves on edge and as taut as a tightly stretched piece of wire. 'What exactly are you trying to say?'

His features hardened measurably. 'As it stands, Rebecca's records will show she has committed and been charged with a criminal offence,' Nicolas outlined pitilessly. 'Something that will be a detrimental factor in whatever career she chooses to undertake.' His eyes held hers with a dark, unwavering scrutiny. 'Having talked to Rebecca at length, I am assured by her that her ambition lies in entering the medical profession, specialising in paediatrics. A career which involves years of university studies and a degree.'

Kate closed her eyes, then opened them slowly, their deep blue depths becoming shadowed with a haunted hopelessness that was uncontrived.

'Private schooling, clothes, a personal allowance,' Nicolas continued with a chilling softness that sent icy shivers scudding down the length of her spine, 'until she qualifies and becomes financially independent.'

Her eyes seemed locked with his, their expression filled with pain. 'I refuse absolutely to allow Esther to assume financial responsibility for Rebecca.'

His eyes seemed to sear right through to her soul. 'Has it not occurred to you that *I* might choose to become Rebecca's benefactor?'

It took tremendous strength of will to maintain a degree of civility, but she managed it. 'At what price, Nicolas?'

His expression was resolute, and only a fool would fail to detect tensile steel beneath the dangerous smoothness of his voice. '*You*. Reinstated in my home, as my wife.'

CHAPTER THREE

KATE felt her face drain of colour, and despite the warmth of central heating there seemed to be ice coursing through her veins. 'You can't be serious?'

'Very.' A muscle tautened along the edge of Nicolas's jaw, and his eyes darkened with smouldering bleakness.

'*Why*?' The single query held a wealth of agony, and she rose to her feet, like a hunted animal searching for some form of escape.

His gaze became hooded, his voice implacable and undeniably deadly in its intent. 'Accept that it suits me.'

'*No*.' To even consider it was an aberration of her sanity, for she doubted her ability to survive.

The intensity of his gaze nailed her figuratively to the wall. 'So adamant, Kate?' His eyes seemed to destroy every barrier she'd erected in self-defence. 'Can you, in all conscience, deny your sister?'

Instant kaleidoscopic images of a future where Rebecca continued to rebel permeated her brain with vivid clarity. 'Not everyone is fortunate enough to realise their ambition,' she rationalised, knowing she was clutching at straws but determined not to give in easily.

Nicolas assessed every one of her features, taking his time, and when he returned his gaze to hers she had forcibly to control herself from shivering.

'It need not apply in Rebecca's case.'

She flashed him an angry glance, hating him more in that precise moment than she had imagined possible. 'Why choose emotional blackmail to resurrect a marriage that was doomed from the very start? It didn't work then, and it can't work now.'

'So certain, Kate?'

'*Yes*, damn you!' Without thought the words tumbled from her lips. 'I could divorce you and use the financial settlement for Rebecca's education and career.'

His gaze never wavered, and she held it with increasing difficulty, compelled by the conflict raging within to shift her attention slightly to the definitive slope of his patrician nose out of fear of what she might detect in those dark, inscrutable depths.

'Aren't you forgetting an important factor?' His voice held a steely intonation that sent ice scudding down the length of her spine. 'I have the power to delay indefinitely any legal proceedings you instigate in negotiating such a settlement. Years,' he elaborated silkily. 'By the time it could all be resolved, Rebecca would be well into her twenties, and way beyond her present aspirations. Besides,' he continued with deadly softness, his smile a mere facsimile, 'I want children. With you as their mother.'

No! she agonised silently. Then she'd be tied to him forever, torn between a sense of love and loyalty, unable to subject any child of hers to the heart-wrenching débâcle of divorce.

'What you're suggesting is impossible!'

One eyebrow rose fractionally. 'Procreation from an act of lovemaking?'

His masked cynicism brought a rush of colour to her cheeks. 'You know very well what I mean!'

'Elucidate, Kate,' Nicolas drawled. 'I'm curious to hear your detailed objections.'

With quick jerky movements she rose to her feet. She was so angry that she was almost shaking with it. 'Money doesn't give you the right to take control of my life.'

'*Money*,' he elaborated with delicate emphasis, 'will assure Rebecca's future, and ensure she lives in a comfortable home, is given a generous allowance, travels, and leads an enviable social existence.'

His smile didn't reach his eyes, and Kate thought wildly that he resembled a jungle animal stalking its prey; moving in a slow, mesmeric circle as he closed in for the kill, with no doubt in his mind of the conclusion.

'What about *me*?' she cried out in passionate demand. 'Don't my feelings count for anything?'

With easy economy of movement he got to his feet, closing the short distance between them, and her eyes became riveted to his compelling features as he reached out a hand and caught hold of her chin.

'Believe I have your best interests at heart.'

Her eyes warred angrily with his. 'How can you say that?'

His expression hardened fractionally. 'Think carefully before you burn any figurative bridges,' he warned silkily, and she felt the chill of fear invade her veins at his determined resolve.

'I need to give it some thought.'

'The alternatives are remarkably clear,' he intoned with hard inflexibility. 'Yes, or no, Kate.'

No matter how many words she bandied, or for how long, the end result would involve her capitulation. Defeat—*hers*—was a foregone conclusion. Familial loyalty was so deeply ingrained in her psyche that she *couldn't* walk away from Rebecca, any more than she could choose a path that would lead to her sister's destruction. Yet she wasn't prepared to give in without attempting to gain some advantage.

'If I do agree, there's something I require from you.'

'Elaborate, Kate.' His voice was velvet-smooth, yet denoting a will of tensile steel.

'Your fidelity,' she told him. Her eyes became enmeshed with his, and she couldn't tear them away.

He was silent for a few seemingly long seconds, and she held his gaze fearlessly, frighteningly aware of his strength and sense of purpose.

His fingers shifted, sliding through her hair to cup her nape, and for one breathtaking moment she was unclear of his intention, aware only of his close proximity and the dramatic pull of her senses.

Sexual magic. As damningly cataclysmic as it had ever been, she groaned silently. Her body seemed to possess a will entirely of its own, with every single nerve-end quivering into vibrant life in recognition of his powerful alchemy.

A faint sound penetrated her subconscious, forcibly returning her to reality, and she twisted out of his grasp, her startled gaze held by the sight of her sister pushing an elegant tea-wagon resplendent with silver tea service, coffee-pot, milk, cream, sugar, a selection of speciality cakes, which Mary Evans was renowned for providing.

A hesitant, extremely nervous Rebecca, whose lengthy absence in the kitchen had undoubtedly been contrived.

'You didn't eat much dinner,' Rebecca ventured, sending her sister a pathetically appealing glance. 'I know you don't like drinking coffee at night, so I made you some tea.' Her gaze shifted to Nicolas, then switched back to Kate in desperation. 'Is everything all right?'

If you're going to go through with this, Kate determined, start as you mean to go on. Inside, she felt as if her nerves were shredding into a thousand pieces, and she longed to cry out against a fate that would see her reunited with a man she'd sworn never to see again.

'Nicolas and I have been——' Kate paused, then continued with delicate emphasis '—negotiating, for want of a better word.' She contrived a faint smile, and failed miserably.

Rebecca looked from one to the other of them with an expression of glazed agony.

'Successfully,' he drawled tolerantly, and Rebecca's sigh of relief was a palpable sound in the spacious room.

'I don't know what to say,' the younger girl said shakily. 'Or how to thank you.'

'You could pour my tea.' Kate felt as if she needed something to soothe her nerves, and she sank into a nearby chair, watching with detached fascination as Rebecca complied, then she accepted the cup, added sugar, and sipped the hot sweet brew. Her headache was now a throbbing entity, and she lifted trembling fingers to one temple in an effort to ease the pain.

The action drew Nicolas's narrowed glance, and she placed her empty cup on a nearby table. The longing to escape him, even temporarily, was paramount.

'If you don't mind, I'd like to go to bed.'

'By all means,' Nicolas concurred smoothly. 'Mary has prepared the guest suite at the end of the hall for Rebecca.'

Kate assimilated the words, and their implication by deliberate omission. Her eyes clouded with angry deep-seated resentment as she glimpsed the dark, vaguely taunting cynicism evident in his gaze. She opened her mouth, then closed it again in deference to Rebecca's presence.

'Goodnight.' The word escaped her lips in stiff syllables, and she couldn't even bear to look at him as she walked from the elegant room, dimly aware of Rebecca's voice, closely followed by Nicolas's murmured response.

Kate had almost reached the top of the gently curving staircase when Rebecca caught up with her, and she continued on to the landing before turning to face her sister.

For a moment there was a strained silence—one Kate found almost impossible to break in her present frame of mind. Innermost was a desire to begin a series of recriminations, yet the words and their resultant effect were too much for her to cope with at the moment.

'Kate,' Rebecca began hesitantly, her eyes widening at the sight of her sister's pale features, 'are you OK?'

She wanted to scream out an emphatic *no*. To demand if Rebecca had any conception of the effect her actions would have on Kate, personally.

'It's been a very long day,' she managed carefully. 'In more ways than one.' Her lower lip shook slightly, and she caught the inner tissues between her teeth to prevent any visible sign of her fragility.

Rebecca's eyes slowly filled with tears, and in an unbidden gesture she reached forward and hugged Kate's slim form, then quietly wept as Kate's arms slowly linked together at the younger girl's waist.

Then they drew apart, and Kate adjured quietly, 'Go on to bed. We'll talk in the morning.'

Rebecca gave a reluctant nod, then turned and walked to the end of the hall, while Kate moved slowly in the opposite direction.

The master bedroom suite was exactly the same, she determined dully as her eyes swept slowly round the large room, discovering that her suitcase had been placed on the elegant damask-covered stool at the base of the huge bed.

Presumably on Nicolas's instructions, Kate decided, feeling incredibly angry with the man who had wrought such havoc with her life more than three years ago, and who seemed certain to cause turmoil all over again.

It isn't *fair*, she raged inwardly, helplessly caught in a tangled net of circumstances in which only she was the victim.

Yet if she was to be imprisoned in a renewed marriage of mutual convenience then this *home*, with its visual trappings of Nicolas's wealth, was undoubtedly a gilded prison.

Soft pearl-grey deep-piled carpet, cream silk-covered walls with the slightest tinge of pink, exquisite rosewood furniture in a delicate carved design, and a king-sized bed covered in heavy silken damask of varying shades of grey, pink, and amethyst, with an adjoining *en suite* decorated in soft grey tiles with marble fittings in pink and cream.

Nothing had been changed, not even the placing of a few favoured ornaments, or the beautiful watercolour print she'd loved on sight and promptly bought only weeks after she and Nicolas had returned from their honeymoon in the Bahamas.

Turning slowly, Kate wandered towards the door leading into a large connecting room that had originally served as a nursery.

Long since redecorated, it had been used by Nicolas as a dressing-room prior to their marriage, and afterwards it had become her retreat, furnished as a feminine sitting-room complete with escritoire, portable television and a comfortable sofa.

'Curious?' a deep voice drawled from behind. 'Or merely reluctant to re-enter our marriage-bed?'

Kate felt a *frisson* of apprehension slither across the surface of her skin, and her heart began a quickened thudding beat as she turned round to face him.

He stood a few feet distant, his suit jacket hooked over one shoulder, his tie loosened, and the top button unfastened on his immaculate white shirt.

He looked infinitely dangerous, his broad-chiselled features curiously still, his eyes watchful and incredibly dark.

'Both,' Kate reiterated, casting him a look of calculated indifference.

'You'll sleep here in this room, with me,' Nicolas insisted with silky detachment. 'Any histrionics, real or imaginary, will have no effect whatsoever.'

A well of rage rose up inside her, the force of it causing her to sway slightly on her feet, and her eyes sparked blue fire as she curled the fingers of both hands into tightly clenched fists. 'You—*barbarian*,' she whispered vehemently. 'Can't you at least have the decency to wait a few nights before——?'

'Insisting on the resumption of conjugal rights?'

'*Yes*, damn you!'

His expression didn't change, and she longed to lash out at him physically in an attempt to expiate some of her anger.

'The wedding-ring you left behind is in the top drawer of the bedside pedestal,' he informed her with pitiless disregard. 'Put it on.'

She opened her mouth to refuse, then closed it again as she glimpsed the chilling sense of purpose evident in those dark eyes.

'I have a few hours' work ahead of me in the study.' Turning slightly, he hung up his jacket, then moved with easy, lithe strides from the room.

She longed to run after him and *slam* the door shut with resounding force, except her limbs seemed weighted and refused to obey the dictates of her brain.

A few minutes later she crossed to the *en suite*, extracted two pain-killing tablets and washed them down with some water, then she unpacked the contents of her bag, slipped into a nightshirt, and stood hesitantly in the middle of the room.

The wide bed looked so inviting, so darned comfortable, and she was so very tired. Yet she was *damned* if she'd meekly slide beneath the covers and lie waiting for Nicolas to return! Such an action was tantamount to a silent acceptance of every one of his terms.

Without further thought she pulled on a robe, then walked soundlessly into the adjoining sitting-room, where she activated the television before curling up comfortably on the sofa.

After switching channels, she discovered a programme that held her interest for a while before she actively began to fight the overwhelming tiredness that threatened its claim.

Kate was dreaming, cocooned in warmth, captured by a spectacular ray of summer sun as she stood in a beautiful country meadow. There were drifts of flowers, and the air was filled with their sweet perfume as she bent low to pick the blossoms. Then a shadow fell, blotting out the sun, and she turned slowly to discover the source, only to be confronted by the tall figure of a man whose very stature she found infinitely frightening. As his hands reached forward she turned and fled, only to stumble and fall headlong into the grass.

She was fighting, wrestling for her life as she attempted to escape his arms, and she cried out, begging for him to let her go.

'*Dios*,' a deep male voice cursed, penetrating her subconscious.

There was the clicking sound of a switch, and light bathed the room, forcing her into reality and the instant awareness that Nicolas occupied the bed. What was more, he was leaning far too close, and her breath seemed to lock in her throat at the sight of him.

'What in the name of heaven were you dreaming about?'

A menacing dark-haired giant who bore an uncanny resemblance to *you*, she longed to tell him. Except there was something more pressing on her mind. 'How did I get here?'

A relatively foolish question, when it was all too obvious he must have transferred her from the sofa into his bed.

'You sleep-walked,' he revealed, deadpan.

'Never in a lifetime,' Kate denied with subdued certainty, all too conscious of him and the effect he was beginning to have on her nervous system.

'Who were you running from?' he prompted, his eyes darkly inscrutable. 'A nightmarish demon? Or me?'

'Both,' Kate owned with an edge of bitterness, knowing the dream had interwoven her inner fear with reality, and that the demon of her dreams and Nicolas Carvalho were one and the same.

'You seemed intent on an attack,' he drawled, leaning slightly towards her as he lifted a hand to her cheek. 'Quiet little punches, which you refused to allow me to subdue.'

He sounded indolently amused, and she flinched away from the brush of his fingers as he pushed back a stray lock of hair behind her ear.

Her eyes clung to his, defensive, and incredibly vulnerable for an instant, then she was edging away from him, instinctively afraid of what might transpire if she stayed.

'Where do you think you're going?'

Unbidden, the tip of her tongue edged across her lower lip, and she shifted her gaze away from the disturbing sight of broad shoulders and an expanse of chest with its matt of dark curling hair.

'What time is it?' An inane query, and one which didn't fool him in the slightest.

'Just after four,' Nicolas drawled.

'I don't want to stay with you,' Kate said starkly.

'It's too late to change your mind.'

'I meant here, in this bed.'

He examined her features, assessing the bright eyes and flushed cheeks with daunting scrutiny. 'Afraid, Kate?'

'No.' Liar, a tiny voice prompted.

His eyes narrowed, assuming a dangerous hardness that was at variance with the softness of his voice. 'Perhaps you should be,' he warned, trailing his fingers along the edge of her jaw before tracing a path down her throat to the gentle swell of her breast.

Kate momentarily closed her eyes as her body began to respond, and there was nothing she could do to prevent the tell-tale hardening of each burgeoning peak, or the unfurling sensation deep inside that slowly began to radiate a tingling awareness throughout her entire body.

'What are you trying to do?' she whispered, her voice sounding strangled even to her own ears, and she glimpsed a degree of cynicism in his faint smile.

'Do you need to ask?'

Her eyes locked with his, seeing the dark sense of purpose evident, and she began to panic. 'I'll fight you,' she vowed with quiet vehemence. 'Every inch of the way. And afterwards you'll have to live with knowing you resorted to rape.'

'Strong words, Kate,' Nicolas drawled. 'When you know only too well it will take little persuasion to have you begging for my possession.'

'That's not true!'

His eyes were strangely watchful above the indolent smile, and she tore her gaze away from the sensual curve of his mouth. 'Shall I prove you wrong?'

'Go to hell!'

'Still the spitting kitten, *querida*? All claws and ready to scratch, only to succumb and purr in my arms. And afterwards beg for more,' he taunted lazily.

'You're despicable!'

He conducted a leisurely appraisal of her stormy features. 'We once shared something very special.'

'Sex,' she flung in utter fury. '*Lust*,' she elaborated accusingly.

'Not two people so in tune with each other that their lovemaking became a beautiful expression of mutual joy?'

Her eyes became luminous, then clouded with bitter pain for a brief second before her lashes swept down to form a protective veil. 'It was never like that,' she denied shakily.

'No?' His voice was a soft drawl, seductive and infinitely disturbing as his head bent down to hers. 'Perhaps I should refresh your memory.'

With a kind of desperate anguish she attempted to turn away from him, except his lips had already found the vulnerable hollow at the base of her neck and seemed intent on wreaking havoc with her nervous system as he struck a long-neglected chord deep within and began playing it with the skill of a maestro.

Dear lord, how could she be so...malleable? she despaired, fighting against that all too familiar ache that began deep inside her stomach.

His touch seemed to liquefy her bones, and she began to shake as his tongue stroked the rapidly beating pulse.

Aware of all her pleasure spots, he allowed his hand to begin a slow downward path to her breast to caress the tumescent peak into full arousal before trailing his mouth to suckle the sensitised nub shamelessly through the thin cotton of her nightshirt.

Fire coursed her veins like quicksilver, until her whole body was one large, pulsing ache demanding assuagement, and she moved restlessly in an attempt to ease the intensity of feeling deep within her central core.

Almost as if he knew of her anguish, his hand splayed across her stomach in a soothing gesture, then eased gently down to seek the outer moistening dew, caressing, probing, *teasing* with such provocative skill that she began to moan, silently begging him to complete the seduction with his possession and a total satiation of her senses.

Such was her descent into passionate oblivion that she was hardly aware that he removed her nightshirt, and she gave a faint sigh as his mouth closed over her breast to tease its highly sensitised nub with his teeth, frequently bringing her to the brink of pain before retreating to capture its twin and render a similar supplication.

Then, not content, his mouth grazed a destructive path down her rib-cage to savour her navel before slowly traversing her stomach to nurture the most intimate crevice of all.

It was an unbearable torture, and utterly devastating. She felt like a small boat in a storm-tossed sea, almost beyond reason as he pressed gentle bruising kisses to her soft skin in an upward trail towards her mouth.

It began as a gentle possession, filling her senses, then assumed a ravaging devastation that almost destroyed her as he sought to impress his mark.

Just as she thought she could stand it no longer he slowly lifted his head, his eyes impossibly dark as he took in her softly swollen lips, the shimmering sapphire depths brimming with hurtful reproach.

'Don't,' Kate whispered in utter desolation, silently pleading with him. 'Please,' she added, almost begging as the silent tears slowly spilled over and rolled down her cheeks to rest against the curtain of her hair that lay spread out over the pillow.

A spasm shook her slim form, and she closed her eyes, shaking her head in silent self-denial. There were so many words she wanted to fling at him, yet her lips were trembling so badly that she was hardly able to speak, and her hands fluttered helplessly down to her sides.

'Tears,' Nicolas accorded with deadly softness. 'A woman's ultimate weapon.'

With deliberate slowness he lowered his head to hers, and she closed her eyes against the darkness of his gaze, expecting a swift retribution.

Except none followed, and instead she felt his lips trace the path of her tears before brushing across her sensitive mouth to settle momentarily against the hollow at the base of her throat.

With a sense of detached fascination she watched as he reached into the pedestal drawer and retrieved a gold band encrusted with diamonds.

'You forgot something.' Catching hold of her left hand, he slid the ring into place. 'Relax, Kate,' he bade her silkily. 'And sleep—if you can.'

Switching off the light, he settled comfortably, while Kate lay tense and unmoving, hating him just as much as she hated his ability to slip easily into somnolence at will.

It was agony to lie still beside him, and there was no power on earth that would permit her to admit, even to herself, that she was filled with a numbing emptiness so acute that it became a tangible entity, ensuring inability to achieve sleep.

There were too many images torturing her mind, and she stared blankly at the darkened ceiling, summoning every relaxation technique she knew in an effort to slip into a welcome void, except there was no release, and consequently it was almost dawn before she fell into a deep, troubled sleep, from which the housekeeper woke her at eight with a cup of sweetened black coffee.

CHAPTER FOUR

'NICOLAS has already eaten,' Mary Evans informed Kate as she moved to open the heavy curtains. 'He said to tell you he'll be busy in the study until nine, and asked that you and Rebecca be ready to leave for the city at nine-fifteen.' She fastened the curtains, then turned towards Kate with a kindly smile. 'Rebecca is already downstairs. What would you like for breakfast?'

Kate thought rapidly, and decided her stomach wouldn't cope with anything other than the lightest of fare. 'Orange juice, some toast, and coffee, please,' she declared gratefully. 'Give me fifteen minutes.'

The view from the wide picture window was magnificent, taking in the full sweep of the inner harbour with its many coves and inlets, the harbour bridge and the city's many tall buildings shrouded in a light misty haze. It was a beautiful winter's day, clear skies, sunshine, and crisp cool air.

Almost as if the rage of yesterday's windswept rain had never been, Kate reflected idly as she moved quickly into the *en suite* to shower.

Deciding what to wear posed little problem, and she selected a black tailored skirt and multi-coloured handknitted angora jumper. Her hair was something else, and she twisted it into a knot atop her head before discounting the style for an elegant chignon.

The breakfast-room downstairs was delightfully warm due to a combination of central heating and the sun's rays filtering through the floor-to-ceiling tinted-glass windows.

'What do you think, Kate?' Rebecca queried as Kate took a seat at the table. 'Shall I wear a skirt and jumper, or a dress?'

'A dress,' she advised without hesitation as she poured some fresh orange juice into a glass.

'Nicolas has arranged an appointment with the headmistress at four.' She looked unbearably anxious. 'If I'm accepted, when do you imagine I'll be able to start?'

'I have no idea,' Kate responded honestly. The school Nicolas had nominated was one of the most exclusive and expensive private educational institutions in Sydney. Entry into its hallowed halls just had to involve rigid protocol...even given the status of the Carvalho name and its resultant influence.

'You're not——' Rebecca hesitated, then plunged ahead with the insensitivity of extreme youth '—real happy with me right now, are you?'

Oh, lord, how did she answer that? With cautious honesty, Kate decided, pausing from the process of biting into her toast she directed her sister a look that was startlingly level. 'I don't approve of what you've done, or how you've gone about achieving your objective. It surely had to occur to you that I'd be out of my mind with worry?'

'Yes. But it turned out all right, didn't it?'

'You run away,' Kate reiterated with quiet vehemence, 'commit a crime, get arrested by the police, have charges laid against you, and involve the Carvalho family, resulting in me having to strike a bargain with the devil, virtually to save your skin and safeguard your future . . . and you have the gall to pass it off as turning out *all right*?'

'But Nicolas is fantastic,' Rebecca protested with injured innocence. 'I could never understand why you left him, and all this,' she paused to effect an encompassing gesture with both arms, 'in the first place.'

'I don't expect you to,' she said curtly. 'In any case, it's water under the bridge.'

'You don't want to talk about it?'

'No.' She felt tired through lack of sufficient sleep, and acutely fragile. *Bruised*, she amended silently, aware of several faint contusions on her sensitive flesh from Nicolas's touch. Even her breasts felt slightly swollen, their peaks faintly tender against the silk material of her bra, so that almost every movement brought forth a vivid reminder of his seduction.

The thought of having to face Nicolas again, to be forced to act out a part, was more than she could endure. The daylight hours were bad enough, but what about tonight and all the nights that would follow?

'If it means anything,' Rebecca ventured hesitantly, 'I'm sorry.'

Sparing her watch a quick glance, Kate drained her cup and set it back on the saucer. 'It's almost nine. You'd better change, while I put on some make-up.'

Nicolas emerged from the study just as Kate followed Rebecca downstairs, and she forced herself to meet his dark assessing gaze with an equanimity she was far from feeling.

'Ready?' His gaze shifted to Rebecca, and, sensing her nervousness, he proffered a faint smile. 'This morning's appearance in court will be merely a formality.'

'I just hope it turns out the way you expect it to,' Rebecca uttered with subdued solemnity.

The fact that it did owed much to the considerable standing of Nicolas's legal representative, Kate realised several hours later. An adjournment was granted without question, and after a satisfactory lunch, eaten in an inner-city restaurant, Nicolas drove them to keep an afternoon appointment with the school's headmistress, where the Carvalho charm and considerable influence worked a miracle in the successful waiving of protocol—sufficiently to assure Rebecca a place in their ranks, with a request for Rebecca to report at four o'clock on Sunday afternoon, ready for commencement in classes the following day.

It had been, without question, a highly successful day, Kate reflected as the Bentley purred smoothly along the New South Head Road towards suburban Vaucluse.

Rebecca was ecstatic over the outcome of events, and expressed enthusiasm at the thought of spending the next few days shopping and being fitted for the school's uniform.

'Esther will be delighted to accompany you,' Nicolas drawled as he brought the car to a halt in the driveway.

Indoors, he paused to regard them both, his eyes swinging from Rebecca's animated expression to linger on Kate's carefully schooled features. 'I have work requiring my attention in the study. I'll see you at dinner.'

'Thank you, thank you, *thank* you, Nicolas,' Rebecca enthused with youthful exuberance, and she flung her arms around his waist in a completely uninhibited display of affection.

Her head barely reached his shoulder, and Kate felt a sharp stab of envy that was totally at variance with the dictates of her heart. Her eyes widened fractionally as they met Nicolas's penetrating gaze, and she was powerless to prevent the tiny shock waves that emanated deep within in recognition of his devastating sexual alchemy.

It was crazy, she decided shakily. Absolutely insane. Her lashes flickered faintly, and he smiled— a musing, slightly cynical acknowledgement that brought a defiant gleam to the sapphire depths of her eyes.

'I'll make a cup of tea,' she managed calmly. 'And see if Mary needs any help preparing dinner.'

Without a further word she turned and made her way towards the kitchen, aware of a strange prickling sensation between her shoulder-blades. She vaguely registered Rebecca's excited chatter and Nicolas's deeper tones, then a door closed, immediately followed by the sound of light footsteps crossing the tiled entry.

The tea revived her flagging spirits, and, conscious of a restlessness she was unable to explain, she ran lightly upstairs to change into jeans.

A walk in the fresh air might clear her head, and she emerged into the garden to wander along the side-path, admiring the winter blooms, the stalwarts that survived the cold and blustery rain. Carefully tended to within an inch of their lives, the numerous shrubs flourished in their neat beds, and she paused every now and again to touch a satiny leaf.

The rear of the grounds were beautifully landscaped, incorporating a tennis court and swimming-pool, and Kate had vivid memories of several parties held outdoors during her brief year-long marriage to Nicolas, glamorous social events attended by numerous of the city's social élite.

Women, with few exceptions, whose major interest was being seen wearing the latest designer gear and exchanging gossip, Kate reflected a trifle grimly as she traversed the tennis court and made her way towards the swimming-pool. Women with whom she would once again be expected to mingle, and entertain.

Nicolas Carvalho's reconciliation with his estranged wife was guaranteed to stimulate the rumour mill, and she would be courted, dissected and assessed in a bid to discover why three years had elapsed between separation and reconciliation, and what had prompted the end of their estrangement.

Presumably she would be expected to act out a charade, and field each and every skilfully voiced barb with considerable tact and diplomacy.

It wasn't fair, Kate brooded, as she paused beside the elegantly curved, beautifully designed pool. She was merely a pawn—used carelessly by Rebecca in a bid to achieve her own ends, and trapped shamelessly into resuming a lifestyle with a man she purported to hate.

Damn, she cursed softly beneath her breath, un-accountably angry with Rebecca—*Nicolas*. Worse, with herself, for being such a fool. She *should* have let her sister take whatever was coming to her, and told Nicolas to go to hell.

A slight shiver shook her slim frame, and she turned, retracing her steps, and once indoors she went straight upstairs to shower and change for dinner.

It was bliss to stand beneath the spray of steaming water, and she took longer than usual, luxuriating in her liberal use of exquisitely perfumed soap before emerging to towel herself dry.

Choosing what to wear posed a slight problem, as the clothes she'd packed were geared to a tropical climate and not the colder temperatures of a southern winter.

'I had Mary store all of the clothes you left behind in the adjacent bedroom,' Nicolas drawled from behind, and Kate swung round to face him, her hands unconsciously pulling together the edges of her robe. 'Maybe you'll find something there.'

She was aware of her hair caught loosely atop her head, with several tendrils falling free, her freshly cleansed face, and the fact she wore nothing at all beneath the silky robe.

The implication of his words penetrated her conscious mind, and her eyes widened measurably as she studied his arresting features. 'I imagined you would have donated them to a worthy cause.'

One eyebrow rose slightly. 'Removed every visible sign that you had ever occupied my home?'

The fact that he hadn't was infinitely puzzling. 'Why not?' She effected a faint shrug, and lowered her gaze from those compelling dark eyes regarding her with indolent scrutiny. 'You can't have imagined I'd ever return.'

'Yet you have.'

Her fingers caught hold of the ties fastening her robe, relentlessly tightening them as she tilted her chin and held his gaze with fearless disregard. 'Not willingly.'

'Of course not,' Nicolas intoned with hateful ease, and her eyes sparked with brilliant blue fire as she launched into a verbal attack.

'You gave me no option!'

'None whatsoever.'

His cynical response rankled unbearably, and she experienced a renewed sense of helpless anger while struggling with a conscience that demanded she extend him some gratitude.

'Thank you for everything you've done,' she managed in a stilted voice. 'Rebecca is extremely fortunate.'

With an easy movement he shrugged out of his suit jacket and loosened his tie. 'Your innate sense of good manners to the fore?' His eyes speared hers, lancing right through to her soul, and a lazy smile broadened the generous curve of his mouth. 'So—thank me.'

Her heart gave a nervous jump, then settled into a quickened beat. 'I just have.'

'I've something more——' he paused fractionally '—emotionally satisfying in mind.'

His faint mockery was almost her undoing, and she drew a deep, steadying breath. 'Sex?' she demanded, tempering her anger with difficulty. '*Now*?' She even managed a strained laugh. 'Really,

Nicolas,' she chided, forcing herself to subject him to a searching appraisal, noting the strength of purpose evident, the almost primitive sensuality apparent.

It took tremendous effort to drag her eyes away, but she managed, sparing the clock on the bedside pedestal a deliberate glance before swinging her gaze back to his. 'With fifteen minutes before Mary is due to serve dinner, during which time you need to shower and change?' She shook her head in mocking remonstrance, then summoned forth a dazzling smile. 'Surely you could show a little more ... finesse?'

His eyes narrowed fractionally, never leaving hers for a second, and there was a quizzical twist to his smile. 'Brave words, Kate,' he afforded with dangerous softness. 'Will you be so brave a few hours from now?'

A *frisson* of fear manifested itself in the region of her nape and slithered down to the base of her spine. It angered her unbearably to detect the faint humour lurking in the depths of his eyes, and her own assumed an expression of unrelenting defiance. 'Tonight, tomorrow—next week,' she relayed heatedly. 'What difference does it make?'

'No difference at all.'

She wondered at her own foolishness, for he was a skilled player in any game, while she was a mere amateur. Reason prompted she soothe down her resentment and her anger, for anything less would only bring retribution on her hapless head.

Turning away from him, she moved towards the large walk-in wardrobe with the intention of getting changed.

He made no attempt to stop her, and she heaved a sigh of relief as she heard him cross into the *en suite*, followed closely by the sound of the shower.

Her array of clothes hanging in the capacious wardrobe appeared pitifully small, and most, she confirmed grimly, were indeed attuned to a northern tropical climate.

Even with the warmth of central heating, several items had to be discounted, and she hurriedly donned fresh underwear, then pulled on her robe and crossed the hallway into the adjacent bedroom.

Once there, she opened wardrobe doors, then pulled out numerous dresser drawers, surprised to discover that most of the lingerie and some of the clothes she'd left behind had been carefully laundered or dry-cleaned, and stored. *Why*, when most men would have disposed of such feminine possessions within months of a runaway wife's fleeing the matrimonial home? Even one year was a long time, but *three*?

Damn, she cursed silently. Too much introspection was detrimental to her peace of mind.

Without too much conscious thought, she selected a black tailored skirt, and added an exquisite white lacy-knit mohair evening top.

Nicolas had just emerged from the *en suite* as she re-entered the bedroom, and she experienced momentary shock at the sight of him. In the past he had never displayed embarrassment at appearing totally unadorned in the privacy of their own suite, but after a few years' absence she was helpless to prevent the flood of pink that coloured her cheeks, or the swiftness with which she averted her attention.

Were his actions part of a deliberate ploy to emphasise the imminent intimacy of their marriage? Or merely an attempt to unsettle her? Kate deliberated, unaccountably cross with herself for allowing him to get beneath her skin.

Choosing to ignore him, she sat down at the mirrored dressing-table and extracted essential cosmetics. Keeping her make-up to a minimum, she chose merely to highlight her eyes and added a clear pink gloss to her lips before emerging to step quickly into high-heeled black pumps.

'Ready?'

Kate turned, and schooled her features to remain expressionless. An extremely difficult task when intense masculinity emanated from his every nerve and fibre, which, combined with the aroma of his chosen aftershave, activated a chord deep within, heightening her awareness of him. Even the sheath of expensive clothing did little to tame the essential essence of the man, and for one wild, crazy moment she wanted to turn back the clock to the few short weeks soon after their marriage when she'd believed everything between them seemed so right, so incredibly complete, that it was almost a dream. Then reality had reared its ugly head, and the dream had steadily become a nightmare.

'Something bothers you?'

The sound of that indolent faintly teasing drawl brought her sharply back to the present, and she shook her head, forcing herself to meet his gaze with unblinking clarity.

'Nothing. Nothing at all.' Turning towards the door, she preceded Nicolas from the room, supremely conscious of him as they descended the elegant staircase together, and in the lounge she accepted a small glass of wine, sipping it slowly until Rebecca joined them.

Dinner was a convivial meal, doubtless aided by Rebecca's constant chatter about the prospect of a shopping spree over the next few days, her list of uniform requirements, and the excellent amenities at school.

Kate deliberately kept a low profile, and, although there was considerable relief that Rebecca appeared happy and enthused about her future, it was impossible to still the tension gnawing away at each individual nerve-ending.

Nicolas proved an urbane host, treating the meal as a small celebration resulting from Rebecca's acceptance as a boarder into the school of his choice. Certainly the food was superb, from the excellent consommé, beef wellington and assorted vegetables, to a mouth-watering apple pie. Except Kate was only able to face the soup, accepted a small portion from the main course, and declined dessert. After a few sips of wine she discarded the beautifully cut crystal flute for a glass of chilled water, and declined coffee in favour of tea.

With each passing minute she became more frighteningly aware how the evening would end. There was a watchfulness apparent beneath Nicolas's smiling façade, a deceptive mildness that didn't fool her in the slightest.

She retained a vivid memory of Nicolas Carvalho, the man. Though he was incredibly kind to those few who held his affection, she knew him to be utterly ruthless with an adversary, portraying chilling strength of will beneath an air of leashed control.

Combined with undisputed power and dynamic energy, the composite was intensely arresting—and vaguely frightening, Kate acknowledged, aware that any element of fear was based entirely on her own response to his vibrant brand of sexuality.

'I think I'll have an early night. If you'll both excuse me?'

Kate heard Rebecca's words, and immediately the butterflies inside her stomach began a series of somersaults. 'Goodnight,' she managed lightly. 'I'll see you at breakfast.'

As soon as Rebecca had left the room, Kate began collecting cups and saucers, and stacked them on to the mobile tea-wagon.

'Leave those,' Nicolas drawled. 'Mary will see to them in the morning.'

'It'll be easier for her if I load the tea-wagon and take it into the kitchen,' Kate responded, and glimpsed his faint amusement.

'A delaying tactic, Kate?' His voice held a degree of lazy tolerance, and he looked so comfortably at ease, so relaxed, that she had the most absurd desire to ruffle his calm exterior.

'*Yes*, damn you! I don't feel in the least inclined to go meekly upstairs and behave like a dutiful wife in bed.'

'We struck a bargain,' Nicolas drawled with ruthless inflexibility. 'A stable existence for Rebecca, expensive private schooling.' His eyes didn't leave hers for a second. 'In return, I get you.'

'Don't my feelings count for anything?' she burst out in heartfelt defiance.

'Stop erecting obstacles. You must be aware I'll discount each and every one of them.'

'Oh—go to *hell*.' Without warning, her hand swept in an upward arc, only to be caught in a crushing grip an inch from its target.

'Are you sufficiently foolish not to realise how very easily I could consign you there?' His voice was chillingly hard, and she looked at him with stormy eyes as he drew her inextricably close.

'Living with you *is* hell,' Kate flung carelessly. Taut, angry words that bordered close to sheer rage as she glared balefully at him, uncaring in that moment what form his retribution might take.

The atmosphere between them was so highly charged that she almost expected it to ignite into flame.

His eyes flared, and his facial muscles tightened into a mask of silent anger as he lowered his head to hers.

His intention was clearly evident, and she clenched her jaw, then twisted her head in an attempt to avoid his mouth. Except it was way too late, and a silent moan of entreaty rose in her throat as the relentless pressure forced her lips apart.

There was nothing she could do to stop his plundering invasion, and she cried out against the silent agony of a kiss so intense, so damnably possessive, that the muscles of her jaw, her throat, stretched to a level of unbearable pain.

In a desperate effort to get him to desist, she balled her hands into fists, hitting his ribs, his back, anywhere she could connect with, until he shifted slightly, altering his hold so that she was caught up against the length of his body, a virtual prisoner as he pinned her arms together behind her back.

It seemed to go on forever, becoming a ravaging possession that violated all her senses, tumbling her into a vortex of conflagration from which she had no hope of emerging intact.

Then it was over, and she stood still, unable to move as he slowly lifted his head. Her eyes felt huge, their depths a shade of sapphire so dark that they appeared fathomless pools in a face starkly devoid of any colour.

Kate was dying inside, so emotionally and physically spent that if she attempted to move she'd probably fall in a heap at his feet.

Unshed tears pricked the back of her eyes, threatening to spill, and she blinked rapidly to disperse them.

Without a word he placed an arm beneath her knees and lifted her high against his chest, walking from the lounge with easy lithe strides as he headed towards the staircase leading to the upper floor.

Entering the master suite, he closed the door, moving to the middle of the room before letting her slide down to stand in front of him.

Slowly he began divesting her of every item of clothing, his eyes hard and obdurate, deadly in their intent as he discarded his jacket.

Dammit, she *wouldn't* cry, she decided fiercely, nor would she fight. There was no way she'd give him the satisfaction.

For what seemed an age he just looked at her, and she stood mesmerised, almost unable to breathe. Then he reached for her, his head descending as his lips sought the vulnerable pulsing cord at the side of her neck, and she was unable to suppress the faint shiver that shook her slender frame.

'I hate you,' she said in an agonised whisper, powerless to prevent the faint surge of emotional exultation that rose from deep within and made a mockery of her expressed words.

'Hate me as much as you like, little cat,' Nicolas drawled huskily. 'At least it's a healthy emotion, and afterwards it won't matter at all.'

'You might possess my body,' she retaliated vehemently, and her eyes darkened into deep blue pools, 'but never my mind, or my heart.'

'Never is a long time,' he accorded silkily. 'Emotions change. I can't imagine you'll remain unmoved by the miracle of conceiving and giving birth to our child.'

'It will be my child, too,' she reminded him heatedly, and managed to quell the sudden lurch of her heart at the mere thought. 'And I want at least a year before being tied down by the demands of motherhood,' she declared bravely.

His eyes hardened until they resembled polished onyx. 'What if I ask you not to take any medically prescribed precautions?'

'You've called the tune in this marriage,' she responded fiercely. 'Right from the very start, I've had no room to manoeuvre. At least allow me one concession.'

His eyes narrowed, assuming a daunting bleakness that was at variance with the velvet-smoothness of his voice. 'One year, Kate. No more.'

'*Dammit*,' she cried out, almost beyond endurance. 'Who do you think you are, that you can attempt to play God?'

He was silent for several seemingly long seconds. His smile was hard, his eyes obdurate. 'For a predetermined price—Rebecca's benefactor, and ultimately *yours*.'

She was so angry, so incredibly wild with fury, that she lashed out at him, uncaring of any retribution.

There was a feeling of supreme satisfaction when her fist connected with one sinewy shoulder, and she quickly followed the punch with a fist into the hard musculature beneath his chest. In a moment of total madness she aimed for his jaw, and missed as he shifted slightly, then she gave a startled gasp as her momentum carried her forward to sprawl in a heap on the mattress at the foot of the large bed.

Any effort to scramble to her feet proved fruitless as Nicolas leaned forward and captured her hands, and she fought against him, violently threshing her limbs in an attempt to kick free.

'Stop it,' Nicolas commanded, holding her still with such ease that it was positively galling.

'Leave me alone!' It was an impassioned plea which had no effect whatsoever, and she struggled desperately in a bid to escape. Her hands, her feet were held immobile, but she still had one weapon— her mouth, and she used it shamelessly as she sunk her teeth into the sculptured muscle close to his breast.

Kate cried out as his fingers slid carelessly through the length of her hair to her nape, uncaring of the tender roots, then she gave an agonised whimper as his mouth closed over the soft underswell of her breast to render a similar assault that tipped her over the edge as pain arrowed through her body in an excruciating wave.

'You *bastard*,' she accused him in whispered outrage.

Nicolas lifted his head, and his eyes seemed to lance right through to her very soul. 'Are you through playing games?'

'I'm not playing at *anything*!' Shimmering tears of fury filled her eyes, lending her a haunting beauty.

'Then stop fighting me at every turn. You must know you can't win, and in the end you'll only get hurt.'

'I *am* hurt already, damn you!'

'What did you expect?' he queried hardily. 'To attack and not have me retaliate?'

'Go to hell, Nicolas.'

'You're treading dangerous ground, *querida*.'

'Don't call me that!' she cried out, hating his use of the teasing endearment that had once meant so much. There were numerous conflicting emotions swirling inside her head, vying for supremacy with a vivid, haunting memory of their lovemaking.

He was so close, his mouth only inches from her own, and her eyes widened slightly in mesmerised fascination as his head lowered to hers.

For an imperceptible second she tensed, expecting an annihilation, then her lips parted in a protesting gasp as his mouth took possession of her own.

Defenceless and totally enervated, she lay still as he gently probed the tender tissues, seeking out the sensitised contours before retreating to trace the swollen softness of her lips.

It was hopelessly erotic to have his tongue stroke hers, and her body arched slightly as his lips slid down the smooth silken column of her throat to settle in a vulnerable hollow at the edge of her neck.

An electric awareness coursed through her veins, activating her senses until she felt achingly alive and totally boneless beneath the caress of his touch.

It was madness not to protest, and, while one part of her brain urged her to break free, the other luxuriated in the erotic tasting he conducted of her skin as he trailed an explorative path of all the sensitive pleasure spots, slowly and with such infinite care that she cried out his name as his mouth closed over the tautened peak of her breast.

Fire shot through her body, all-consuming as it licked along every ncrve-end, every fibre, until she was melting with a desire so tumultuous that she thought she might actually die if he didn't assuage the demands of her traitorous flesh.

Hardly aware of her actions, she reached out and caught hold of his head, urging it towards her own, her lips seeking his in a kiss he allowed her to initiate before staking a possession that dissolved any vestige of resistance and sent her clinging to him in willing supplication.

With consummate skill he prepared her to accept the full thrust of his masculinity, stilling at her faint gasp before gently completing that initial stroking entry.

Kate caught her breath, her eyes impossibly wide and luminous as he filled her completely. Then hc began to move, slowly at first, until the increasing pace caught her up into a maelstrom of sensation from which she never wanted to descend.

Time became a suspended entity, and it seemed an age before the tumultuous surge of emotion began to lessen, assuming an exotic warmth that left her satiated and filled with languid inertia.

She didn't want it to end, she decided dreamily, loving the soft trail of Nicolas's mouth as it caressed her temple and traced its way down to the edge of her mouth.

She smiled faintly, feeling impossibly shy as firm fingers caught hold of her chin, tilting it so she had to look at him.

Dark slumberous eyes held a mesmerising quality, a liquid warmth from which she instinctively wanted to retreat, and her eyelashes slowly lowered to form a protective veil, only to fly open as his teeth caught hold of her lower lip.

'Don't hide from me, Kate,' he berated gently, and his mouth closed over hers in a kiss that was so incredibly evocative that her eyes began to ache, then fill with tears.

Three years hadn't lessened the wild sweet havoc she experienced in his arms, nor tamed the erotic abandon of her response.

Why, *why* was she so attuned to this one man, so inextricably involved, that their lovemaking became a merging of both soul and spirit?

It hardly made sense that she could actively *hate* him for forcing a reconciliation, then fall so completely prey to an inglorious complexity of primeval emotions and exult with such wanton abandon, held so intently captive in the thrall of his possession.

Part of her wanted such a sensual meshing to be for all of the right reasons, and it saddened her unbearably that what Nicolas had said was true... *afterwards* it really hadn't mattered at all.

Even as the thought filtered through her brain, she suppressed a faint shiver, and the lips that nuzzled the soft curve of her neck stilled, then he shifted, moving to the side of the bed before getting to his feet.

Without a word he caught her into his arms and carried her into the adjoining *en suite*, ignoring her indrawn gasp as he leant down and set about filling the large spa with water.

Minutes later he activated the jets, and the water's surface became a pulsating bubbling mass into which he descended, sitting with ease as he placed her between the cradle of his thighs.

She watched in fascination as he soaped a large sponge, then gently applied it to the curve of her neck, slowly traversing every inch of her skin until she was a mindless trembling mess from the slow torment of his pleasuring.

Kate thought dazedly that he couldn't want her again, and she voiced a token protest, her eyes wide and luminous with the strength of her own desire, only to see the depth of dark slumberous passion evident in his own as he gently positioned her to accept his length.

It was impossibly erotic, and he smiled at her fleeting change of expression, measuring her faint surprise and gradual ascent into exultation with musing indulgence.

He knew precisely how to explore the depths of her sexual being, extracting with seeming ease a response so craven, so impossibly primitive, that it was as if she was part of him, the other half of his soul.

Kate closed her eyes as sensation began to subside, and she gave a faint sigh as his hands shaped her delicate rib-cage, then slid down to cover the concave softness of her stomach, before slipping up to cup the fullness of her breasts. Their peaks were tender, and she unconsciously held her breath as he lowered his head to suckle shamelessly from one, then the other, until she arched away from him in protest, only to gasp out loud as he brought her face down to his, covering her mouth with his own in a kiss that was so impossibly erotic that it almost transcended reality.

A long time later he switched off the jets, released the water, then stepped from the spa to scoop her out to stand before him.

With infinite care he towelled her dry, then held out the large fluffy bathsheet in silent invitation for her to return the favour, his eyes assuming faint amusement as she shook her head.

'No?' White teeth gleamed as a faint tinge of pink coloured her cheeks. Without a word he completed the task, then he lifted her into his arms. 'Bed, my sweet Kate. This time to sleep, hmm?'

Nestled in the warm cocoon of his possessive embrace, she fell into a deep, untroubled somnolence, only to wake before the first light of dawn, disturbed by the feather-light touch of his lips as they gently tasted the soft smoothness of her cheek, and this time their lovemaking assumed a wild, untamed quality that left her feeling acutely vulnerable.

It was almost as if three years' absence had been dismissed as something of little consequence now that a reconciliation had been effected.

Yet she couldn't just slip into a seemingly comfortable relationship. She *couldn't* allow herself to be lost in the anonymity of merely being an appendage to Nicolas Carvalho. A charming social hostess who was given a generous allowance in return for her sexual favours.

Four years ago she'd accepted his terms, because she'd had little option. The one mistake she'd made, she allowed with slight bitterness, was to fall into the trap of believing lovemaking had everything to do with *love*.

Now Nicolas would discover he possessed an exemplary wife, and no one would guess that their reconciliation was anything other than what it was purported to be.

As Kate Carvalho she would excel, and *revenge* would be very sweet.

CHAPTER FIVE

ESTHER was a veteran when it came to shopping, and she knew precisely what suited, and what didn't. Once Rebecca's school uniforms had been taken care of, they had simply been driven by Sebastian to the exclusive suburb of Double Bay, at which point, on Esther's instructions, he was to return home. They would, she declared, not need him until at least five o'clock.

The Carvalho name and known wealth, combined with Esther's genuine charm, were sufficient to elicit personal service from the manageress of every establishment in the select collection of Double Bay boutiques.

Rebecca was in her element, and Kate began to protest as Esther seemed intent on almost completely refurbishing the young girl's wardrobe.

'Enough, Esther,' she declared as they waited for Rebecca to emerge in a gown Esther had insisted be brought for their approval.

'Nicolas,' Esther declared, her eyes bright with enjoyment, 'issued precise instructions. *You*, my dear, are next.'

'Am I, indeed?' she queried, feeling the familiar surge of anger at her husband's apparent arrogance.

'Darling Kate,' her mother-in-law chastised with a gentle smile, 'Nicolas leads a very high-profile existence. There are numerous functions and social events he is expected to attend. It's essential you have an up-to-date wardrobe.' She reached out and patted Kate's hand. 'Think of it as an investment.'

Some investment, Kate decided several hours later when she slid wearily into the rear seat of the Bentley. There were several thousand dollars' worth of purchases stored in a variety of packaging reposing in the boot of the car. Esther had been indefatigable, with Rebecca as her willing ally.

Sebastian negotiated the early evening traffic with care, then, after depositing Esther at her doorstep, he continued home.

'I'm going to have the longest shower,' Rebecca declared as they made for the staircase.

'And I intend to soak for ages in the spa,' Kate informed her.

'Today was marvellous, wasn't it?' the younger girl enthused, and on reaching the top of the stairs she turned and gave Kate an impulsive hug. 'Oh, Kate, I'm so glad we're here. All those wonderful clothes, a fabulous school. Nicolas is——'

'A fairy godfather?'

Rebecca looked faintly startled for a few seconds at her sister's faint air of cynicism. 'You can't prefer Antonio's cottage to *here*?'

'Go and have your shower,' she bade her quietly, unwilling to enter into a discussion regarding her sister's estimation of Nicolas's exalted position. 'Dinner is at six-thirty.'

In the master suite Kate quickly crossed into the *en suite* and ran water into the capacious spa, then she discarded her clothes, activated the jets, and stepped into the pulsing water.

The relaxing effect was total bliss, Kate reflected as she closed her eyes and let the warm, delicately scented water ease some of the day's tension from her body.

What she wouldn't give to forgo dinner and retire to bed, *alone*. Except her diabolical husband would never allow it, she decided wryly.

Nicolas was a law unto himself. Obdurate, implacable, and utterly ruthless on occasion.

She suppressed a faint shiver as she recalled the skilled ease with which he'd dispensed with each and every one of her protestations, staking his claim in a manner that left little doubt as to how he expected their marriage to continue.

It would be *years* before Rebecca reached financial independence, she agonised in despair, painfully aware that she was caught in a trap, securely bound, this time, by a familial tie she found impossible to break.

A slight sound disturbed her thoughts, and her eyes flew open to see the object of her ruminations standing a few feet distant.

'What the hell do you think you're doing?'

'Sharing your bath,' he drawled, and she was so incensed that she picked up a sponge and *threw* it at him, watching in scandalised silence as he removed his briefs then lowered his lengthy frame into the spacious spa to sit within touching distance.

'Damn you,' she cursed vengefully. 'Am I not to be permitted any privacy at all?'

His eyes assumed a dark, lazy tolerance as they regarded her ill-concealed fury. 'My dear Kate, I can't imagine anything more relaxing than sharing a spa with my wife after a long day at the office.'

She wanted to lunge at him in fury and launch a physical attack. 'What about *my* long day, walking hard pavements in high-heeled shoes?' she retorted angrily. Her eyes flashed blue fire as she shot him a furious glare. 'My feet hurt, my legs ache—*everything* aches!' she concluded with deliberate ambiguity.

All day she'd been conscious of the faint pull of little-used muscles, acutely aware of tender tissues still sensitive from this man's possession after three years of celibacy.

Almost to the point where she could *feel* his imprint inside her, and he knew, damn him! She could see the lurking knowledge, the recognition in the depths of his eyes, and she hated him afresh.

'Was it so bad, Kate?' he drawled hatefully, the lines arrowing away from the corners of his eyes deepening with ill-concealed humour as he saw the faint tinge of pink colour her cheeks.

'You behaved like an insatiable *animal*,' she accused him angrily. 'I hated every minute of it—every *second*!'

'Would you have preferred me to show little desire for the woman I chose as my wife?'

Her head reared back, her eyes wide with resentment as she denied, 'You never *chose* me, Nicolas.' The truth of their union rose up like bitter gall in her throat. 'Not the first time. Not now.'

'I married you.'

She felt a pain pierce the region of her heart, so acute that she momentarily held her breath, her eyes becoming impossibly dark as she fought for control. 'Yes,' she agreed shakily. 'And neither of us is under any illusion as to *why*.' All of a sudden she'd had enough, wanting only to escape from his disturbing presence.

Yet before she could stand Nicolas caught hold of her right foot, holding it securely as she attempted to wrench it from his grasp.

His gaze speared hers. 'Relax.'

'How can I *relax*?' Kate retaliated as he began a soothing massage of her instep, the tendons at her ankle, before working magic on her calf muscles.

It felt so good, so darned therapeutic, that it would be all too easy to close her eyes and simply *enjoy*. Except that was a danger she could ill afford.

'Let me go.'

'When I've finished.'

Without thought, she kicked at him with her left foot while attempting to free her right, only to find both ankles encased in a firm grip. 'Dammit, Nicolas—let me go!'

'Afraid, Kate?'

'Can't you at least wait a few hours until we go to bed?' Her eyes flashed brilliant blue shards that were meant to spear him right through the heart. 'A seduction scene in the spa within thirty minutes of dinner isn't my ideal path to sexual satisfaction.'

She expected anger, and was infuriated when the grooves slashing each cheek seemed to deepen and lengthen with humour. His husky laugh proved her undoing, and she launched at him in fury, attacking him with flailing fists as she beat his shoulders, his arms—anywhere she could connect with.

With considerable ease he held her immobile. 'I could ring down and have Mary hold dinner,' Nicolas drawled.

Sensation unfurled deep within, together with a terrible feeling of apprehension. 'And risk Rebecca coming looking for us?'

'Oh, I'm sure your sister possesses a sufficiently vivid imagination to be able to deduce the correct reason for our delay.'

Kate closed her eyes, then slowly opened them again. 'Stop baiting me.'

'You rise so beautifully that I find it almost impossible to resist.' His eyes left hers and trailed slowly down the length of her body, darkening slightly as he caught sight of the numerous smudges inflicted during their tempestuous lovemaking.

'Have you no shame?' she queried shakily.

'None at all where you're concerned.'

He released her, and she stepped quickly out from the spa, reaching for a towel to wrap tightly around her slim form, aware that he followed and hitched a towel about his hips.

Kate felt on edge, supremely conscious of his proximity, yet strangely defiant beneath the intensity of his gaze.

She looked at him for a seemingly long time, hating him, yet at the same time terribly afraid of the mesmeric power he emanated. 'You let me go once,' she said in desperation.

'There was never a day when I didn't know your precise whereabouts.'

Kate's mobile features registered an entire gamut of emotions, not the least of which was angry resentment.

'What if I'd filed for a legal separation?' she queried, severely shaken.

'I would have used any means at my disposal to force a reconciliation.'

'*Why*?'

He looked at her in silence, then ventured silkily, 'There was never any doubt our marriage would resume, Kate. The only question was *when*.'

'That's—barbaric,' she whispered, and glimpsed the dark inscrutability in his eyes before her gaze slid down to catch the faint cynical twist of his lips. 'You only married me out of a sense of duty. To my mother—*yours*.'

He reached out and pushed a stray tendril of ash-blonde hair back behind her ear, then brushed his fingers across her cheek. 'Is that what you think?'

Her eyes were wide and unblinking as she searched his features for a visible sign that would provide her with an answer. Except there was none, only a careful watchfulness she found impossible to penetrate.

'I should get ready for dinner,' Kate declared, feeling faintly breathless, and his lips curved in a slow, gentle smile that was infinitely mesmeric.

Without a further word she stepped across the tiled floor to a set of vanity drawers and cupboards, which held her small collection of toiletries.

Her hands shook slightly as she completed her toilette, for she was more emotionally shaken than she cared to admit by his words. Minutes later she escaped into her dressing-room, where she donned fresh underwear and selected clothes at random. Make-up was kept to a minimum, and she chose merely to highlight her eyes with shadow and mascara, then added clear pink gloss to her lips before slipping into high-heeled shoes.

Kate was acutely conscious of Nicolas's presence, intensely aware of his watchful scrutiny as he stood waiting to accompany her downstairs, and it was a relief to escape the implied intimacy of the bedroom.

Dinner was a convivial meal, during which Rebecca took great pleasure in informing her brother-in-law of the extent of their shopping excursion.

'Tomorrow Esther is having a rest,' Rebecca revealed. 'Sebastian is dropping Kate and me at Double Bay. The boutiques there are fantastic.' A faint shadow momentarily crossed her expressive features. 'We're spending an awful lot of money.'

'Esther is planning a dinner party Saturday night as a "welcome home" to you both,' Nicolas declared with indolent ease. 'It will be a formal affair with several guests.'

The food was excellent, but Kate merely forked a few morsels into her mouth, then pushed the food around the plate, her appetite gone.

It was beginning already. The social treadmill of countless dinners, parties, the opera, the theatre, charity functions. Present at such events were the usual social glitterati, the society felines who attended merely to be seen as well as to hear the latest gossip. Kate had hated the artificiality of it all, the bitchiness. Now she was about to be flung into the figurative lion's den again. Had she gained sufficient maturity to cope? And what of Elisabeth Alderton? Was *she* still in evidence?

'Kate, you're not eating. Aren't you feeling well?'

Rebecca's voice intruded on her reverie, and she proffered a faint smile. 'I'm fine. Just not hungry, that's all.'

'You hardly ate a thing at lunch,' Rebecca continued. 'Even Esther commented on it.' Turning towards Nicolas, she offered, 'Kate is too thin, don't you think?'

Kate shifted her gaze to her indomitable husband, and silently dared him to comment.

'A few essential kilos would be an improvement,' he drawled in agreement.

In a minute she'd lose her temper. 'I'm not a child who needs to be tempted with food, and I'll thank you both if you'll stop discussing me as if I were a chicken to be plumply fed for the dinner table.'

Nicolas forked a morsel from his plate and proffered it to her. 'Try some of this.'

'Mary's *pilaf* is divine, Kate,' Rebecca cajoled.

With adroit ease, Nicolas skilfully redirected Rebecca's attention for the remainder of the meal, although Kate was supremely conscious of his faintly narrowed gaze. Consequently it was a relief to escape into the lounge for coffee, and afterwards Nicolas excused himself on the pretext of paperwork requiring his attention in the study.

'Tomorrow we'll concentrate on choosing something really fantastic for you to wear on Saturday night,' Rebecca declared. Her eyes sparkled with anticipation, and Kate had to admit it had been ages—*years* since she'd seen her sister so happy. Gone was the perpetual air of petulance, the antagonism. In its place was pleasure and a glow of contentment.

Although why shouldn't Rebecca be happy? As a result of her own actions, she was now exactly where she wanted to be. It was Kate who paid the price in this débâcle, not Rebecca, and it was impossible not to feel a deep-seated resentment that she'd been given no choice.

'I know just the place,' Rebecca continued with enthusiasm. 'Everything is shockingly expensive, but utterly divine. We'll go there first, shall we?'

Nicolas's wealth precluded a need for cautious spending, and she was sorely tempted to hit back at him through a number of expensive bills.

Kate's smile was a fraction too bright as she rose to her feet. 'If you don't mind, I'll go up to bed. Sleep well.'

It was barely nine, but she felt utterly enervated, and welcomed the thought of slipping between electrically warmed sheets and sinking into merciful oblivion.

At some stage through the night she stirred, then settled again, only to come sharply awake at the realisation that she was no longer alone. Held firmly into the curve of Nicolas's body, she was aware of a hand splayed across her stomach, while the other rested possessively over one breast.

Was he asleep? She tensed slightly, listening to the steady beat of his heart, his deep rhythmic breathing.

'Afraid to move, Kate, for fear I might pounce?' His voice was a husky drawl close to her ear, and his breath teased the hair at her temple.

'You woke me.' It was an accusation rather than a protest, and her body unconsciously stiffened as his hand traversed her hip, then slid down to rest on her thigh. Her breast burgeoned beneath the light brush of his fingers, and she gave a faint gasp as his lips began an evocative teasing tracery of her temple. 'Don't,' she begged, all too aware of the answering response of each and every one of her sensory nerve-endings. 'I don't think I could bear it.'

His lips touched each eyelid in turn, then slid slowly, irrevocably, down to the edge of her mouth.

'Nicolas——' She was drowning, adrift in a sea of her own emotions, his lips an unbearable flame as they tasted her own, savouring the soft outline with such evocative sensuality that she began to melt inside. His open-mouthed kiss became infinitely persuasive, making a mockery of her protest, and it took tremendous strength of will to drag her mouth away.

'No.' She drew air into her lungs in deep, ragged gulps, and her hands pushed ineffectually at his shoulders. '*No.*' His expression was impossible to determine in the darkness, and she took advantage of his stillness to rush into stumbling speech. 'You can't expect me to switch on in bed like a wind-up doll. I have feelings . . .'

She trailed off miserably, and heard his faintly teasing drawl, 'So have I.'

'Lust,' Kate flung, choking back the silent heartache of *years*.

'If that were my sole motivation I'd satisfy my needs without a thought to yours.'

A faint shiver shook her slim frame, and she moved restlessly, lifting her hand then letting it fall in a gesture of helplessness. 'So much has happened in the past few days that I'm not ready for all of this.' For *you*, she added silently.

'You're complaining because I find you desirable?'

There was a tinge of mockery evident that merely strengthened her resolve. 'I'm tired, Nicolas,' she said wretchedly. 'Can't I take a rain-check?'

'And tomorrow, Kate? And the night after that?' His voice sounded like silk being razed by steel. 'Will you proffer one excuse after another in an attempt to deny me?'

'Do I have to pay *every* night?' she queried with such incredible sadness that she had to bite her lip against the aching tears held severely in check. She felt hollow inside, bereft, almost as if part of her had died.

He shifted slightly, settling his length beside her, and she momentarily closed her eyes as he resumed his possessive hold. 'Go to sleep, Kate,' he bade her with musing indolence.

She lay still in an attempt to regulate her breathing, and her eyes ached with suppressed tears long after his deep, rhythmic breathing indicated that he, at least, was unaffected by the emotional turmoil raging within her body.

It was mad—*insane*, but her whole being *ached* for him, every sensory pleasure point screaming out in silent agony for his touch, the assuagement only he could provide.

A long time—*hours*—later she drifted into a restless sleep where dark-haired devils chased her down numerous dark alleys until she eventually reached one from which there was no escape.

On the point of becoming captive, she woke, visibly trembling from the stark vividness of something that only seconds before had seemed so real that she still felt its frightening impact.

'Are you fighting me or some nightmarish facsimile?'

Kate heard Nicolas's soft, musing drawl, and at that precise moment she didn't care that she professed to hate him. All that mattered was a desperate need to forget, and she offered no resistance as he gathered her close in against him.

Her arms crept over his shoulders to link together at his neck, and when his lips sought hers she instinctively opened her mouth, exulting in the firm pressure of his as he led her slowly and with infinite care towards the fulfilment she craved.

'Kate—*yes*,' Rebecca enthused, her eyes sparkling with approval as Kate emerged from the dressing-room of the exclusive boutique. 'The colour, the style—it's perfection.' Her head tilted to one side. 'Turn round,' she bade her, intent as Kate completed a slow circle.

The deep red woollen suit was an excellent foil for her ash-blonde hair and creamy skin, the short skirt hugging her thighs, accentuating their delicate shape, and the beautifully cut long-sleeved jacket defined her narrow waist.

'Don't even hesitate.'

Nicolas would expect her to fit a required image, and, while part of her felt appalled at the staggering amount she was adding to his charge account, the other part urged her to have no compunction whatsoever.

There was already an admirable collection of multicoloured carrier-bags in Rebecca's safe-keeping, the result of several hours' shopping: two evening gowns, three cocktail dresses, shoes, Kate reflected dazedly. Yet the suit *was* perfect. Without a word, she changed into her own clothes, then produced Nicolas's charge card.

'Let's put these in the car,' she suggested as soon as they reached the pavement. 'Then,' she added firmly as Rebecca paused in front of yet another boutique window, 'we're going to have lunch.'

'After which,' her sister declared with youthful enthusiasm, 'we're both going to have a facial, and get some professional assistance in selecting you an entire range of make-up.'

'I don't need——'

'You *do*,' Rebecca insisted with a determined gleam in her eye. 'Eyeshadow, liner, mascara. Not to mention blusher, and a range of lipsticks. Trust me.'

'*Lunch*,' Kate insisted. 'Then I'll give it some consideration.'

The car was parked a few blocks distant, and as they drew close Kate couldn't help but view the Mercedes's gleaming metallic paintwork with a faintly jaundiced eye. Nicolas had casually dropped the keys into her lap as he had left for the city, declaring that she'd need transport of her own. An hour later she'd entered the garage to find the car was nothing less than a superbly styled top-of-the-range SL coupé. Rebecca, with typical exuberance, had let out a whoop of excitement and immediately slid into the passenger-seat.

Now Kate placed the variety of carrier-bags in the boot before turning to retrace their steps to a small coffee shop, which served delicious food and divine capuccino coffee.

'Bliss,' Rebecca sighed as she finished the last morsel on her plate. 'Shall I order another coffee?'

When it was served, Kate sipped the frothy brew and contemplated the ramifications of being thrust back into the social scene. Dinner with Esther, Rafael and their guests on Saturday evening would merely be the first of many such occasions, and she wondered idly how she would cope with the inevitable curiosity regarding her sudden return to Sydney and reinstatement into Nicolas Carvalho's household.

'Come on, Kate. Let's indulge in a pampering session. Tomorrow——'

'Tomorrow,' Kate said firmly, 'we are staying home to attach name-tags to all your school clothes. Then we'll run a check-list in case there's anything we've forgotten. A quiet, relaxing day, Rebecca,' she warned. 'Followed by a relatively early night. Saturday is bound to be late.'

'OK, OK,' Rebecca agreed, spreading her hands in a gesture of accepted defeat. 'I'm not arguing.' She got to her feet with easy grace, and proffered a wide dimpled smile. 'The beauty salon. I want to see what a beautician can do to turn your obvious good looks into something of dazzling attraction.'

'Whom am I supposed to *dazzle*?'

Rebecca's smile widened into something resembling downright devilment. 'Why—*Nicolas*, of course.'

CHAPTER SIX

SATURDAY proved to be a typical mid-winter day, with strong blustery showers that lashed the house and showed little sign of abating as the afternoon progressed.

Esther had insisted they arrive early, and shortly after four Kate entered the *en suite* for a leisurely shower, then she slipped into a robe before tending to her hair.

There was no question of leaving it loose, and she lifted its length high on to her head, tilting it this way and that before twisting it into an elaborate pleat at her nape. Sophistication was the key, she decided as she set about achieving just that image.

All day she had been beset by a nervous tension that seemed to intensify with every passing hour, until it seemed that every nerve-end was on edge, each separate thread tautened to its furthest limitation.

If was crazy to feel so *overwrought*, she determined grimly as she began a second attempt with eyeshadow, eye-liner and mascara. Subtle, understated was the look she contrived. Her fingers shook, and she cursed afresh.

Twenty minutes later she slipped into the exquisite layered rose-petal gauze dress in delicate merging shades of pink, mauve, lavender and grey.

Essentially feminine, it was a dream to wear and accentuated her petite frame.

Matching pink high-heeled shoes completed the outfit, and she stood back from the mirror, reasonably satisfied with her image.

'Ready?'

Nicolas's silky drawl intruded, and she turned to face him, her gaze wide and direct and depicting a determined gleam of intended self-preservation.

His tall frame exuded muscular litheness beneath its sheath of expensive suiting, and she could only envy his projected air of self-assurance. Nothing appeared to ruffle his composure, and she doubted if there had ever been a time when he'd lacked the dramatic mesh of power and elusive sexual alchemy he managed to exude without any effort at all.

For as long as she could remember, he'd stood apart from anyone she'd ever known, possessing the strangest ability to affect her senses. To such an extent that she had assumed the instinctive wariness of a vulnerable doe in the presence of a lazily prowling predator.

Four years ago he'd captured her as prey, holding her for a year before allowing her to slip free. Now he'd permit no such concession. It was there in the darkness of his eyes, the determined set of his jaw, almost as if he sensed her inner struggle and was intent on issuing a silent warning against such folly.

'Yes.' Assertiveness had to be an advantage, Kate decided as she met and matched his level scrutiny. Anything less meant treading a path towards total conflagration.

Conscious of his appraisal, she collected her evening bag, only to pause mid-step as Nicolas held out a coat.

'Slip this on. It's cold outside.'

This was a silver-grey fur in soft luxuriant mink, exquisitely designed and reaching mid-calf.

The movement of her hand was entirely involuntary as she reached out and tentatively trailed her fingers across the beautiful pelt, then she withdrew as if from flame.

Her eyes lifted to encompass his, their depths wide and luminescent beneath the soft overhead light.

'You don't like it?'

The drawled query brought a slight tinge of colour to her cheeks. 'It's beautiful,' she accorded quietly.

'Except you have an obscure reservation.'

He sounded vaguely cynical, and she lifted a hand to her hair in a nervous gesture, touching the pins that held the mass of long ash-blonde curls before letting her hand flutter down to her side, and her eyes assumed a pensive solemnity that wasn't contrived. 'I can't help thinking of all the poor little animals who had to give up their lives for one designer-fashion accessory.'

A faint smile tugged the corners of his mouth, and the grooves slashing each cheek deepened. 'Laudable as your sentiment is, it hardly changes the fact that raising minks solely for the value of their pelts is a highly lucrative industry.'

'I'm not sure I'd feel comfortable wearing such a blatant status symbol.'

'Perhaps you could try,' Nicolas drawled. 'If only to please me.'

Her eyes speared his, darkening into deep sapphire pools. 'And if I choose not to?'

'As a result of strong environmental feelings, or merely as an attempt to oppose me?'

Kate held her breath, then released it slowly. 'What if I said I find it difficult to be beholden to you in any way?'

'You're my wife,' he declared silkily. 'As such, there's no question of your being in my debt.'

Her eyes darkened even further, then flashed blue fire. 'And, as such, I must acquire a certain façade, enabling me to compete with the social élite.'

His gaze conducted a slow analytical appraisal of all her visible features. 'Tell me, do you enjoy being so argumentative?'

'I'm not being argumentative,' she retorted. 'I just don't want to lose my identity!'

His lips parted, and his teeth gleamed white as he regarded her with musing tolerance. 'My dear Kate, I doubt there's any chance of that happening.'

Her eyes assumed a defiant sparkle. 'I don't want to become a society puppet, manipulated by convention to appear at all the right social functions, wearing the latest designer gear, and insulated so thoroughly that I lose track of reality.'

'That's the reason for not accepting a mink coat?'

She was silent for several long seconds, then she drew in a deep breath and released it. 'No!'

His expression sobered into a mask of inscrutability. 'Why not allow your husband to bestow a gift?'

She should capitulate, thank him, and graciously allow him to settle the coat about her shoulders. To battle with him constantly was a fruitless exercise, yet some inner devil pushed her to hold out a little longer.

'What about all the charge accounts I'm running up in your name? Between us, Rebecca and I have spent a fortune these past few days. Or don't they count as gifts, and are merely relegated to a necessity in gilding the figurative lily?'

His eyes narrowed into hard, inflexible brown shards. 'Count yourself fortunate it is my parents we are to visit. Anyone else would not earn a second invitation after the lateness of our expected arrival.'

Apprehension created a painful knot in her stomach, and she cursed herself for behaving like a recalcitrant child. Attempting to thwart him was a wasted effort, and extremely foolish. Her chin lifted fractionally, and her eyes were remarkably clear.

'Another attempt to enforce your superiority and bring about my total submission?' she demanded quietly.

'A statement,' Nicolas reiterated in a hard voice. 'One you'd do well to observe.' He moved forward and placed the coat about her shoulders. 'You *will* wear it tonight, Kate. You may burn it tomorrow for all I care.'

She might well just do that. Without a word, she followed, preceding him into the hallway, then she walked at his side down the elegant staircase to where Rebecca stood anxiously waiting in the lounge.

* * *

The party was an elegant affair, with twenty guests invited to share a sumptuous five-course meal. It was ostensibly an evening to welcome Kate and Rebecca back into the Carvalho family fold, but it soon became apparent that the total focus of everyone's attention was the reason for a reconciliation between Kate and Nicolas Carvalho.

Circumspect conjecture abounded, and Kate found her only defence was to adopt a mask of polite equanimity. Consequently she smiled a lot, conversed with measured reserve, and inwardly reeled beneath Nicolas's solicitous attention.

She began to feel as if she was playing a well-rehearsed part, as his constant presence kept her on edge, and she retaliated to his projected affection by returning it in kind.

'Don't you think you're overdoing this just the tiniest little bit?' Kate murmured as they stood alone together. She proffered him a singularly sweet smile, and kept her eyelashes lowered in an attempt to veil the gleam of anger evident. 'I understand what you're attempting to achieve, but my acting ability is being severely tested.'

'My dear Kate,' Nicolas drawled softly, 'as much as I deplore gossip, I cannot ignore its existence. Would you rather be neglected, and allow conjecture and supposition to run rife?'

'And to think this is only the beginning,' she accorded lightly, knowing that tonight was the first of many social events where she'd be expected to *shine*. 'Why, even Rebecca appears to accept that our relationship has taken a miraculous turnaround.'

'Rebecca is a survivor.'

His voice held quiet cynicism, and she looked at him carefully, the smile widening her lips not mirrored in her eyes. 'And I'm not?'

'Oh, yes.' He reached out and caught hold of her hand to link his fingers through her own. 'Although it is only fair to warn that I have no intention of allowing you to survive without me.'

Kate attempted to wrench her hand free, and failed miserably. 'Let me go, damn you!'

'Careful, my sweet,' he warned softly, and she almost died as his head lowered and he brushed his lips gently across her own. 'Your claws are showing.' Straightening, he lifted her hand and touched his lips to each finger in turn. 'Not much longer until we leave, and once home you can give your temper full rein.'

'At home,' she whispered, so sorely tried that it was a wonder he didn't go up in flames beneath the force of her anger, 'I shall probably do you physical harm!'

His eyes assumed a cynical amusement she found infinitely damning. 'Have you never attempted to analyse *why* you continually fight me?'

The breath caught in her throat, and for one timeless second her eyes were stricken with the strength of her knowledge. 'Because I *hate* you!'

The corner of his mouth twisted with musing mockery as he lowered his head to brush lips to her temple. 'So sure, Kate?'

She tugged at her captured hand, to no avail, then her heart gave a painful jolt as his thumb moved to caress the fast-pulsing veins at her wrist.

It took every ounce of her resolve not to cause a scene, and she hated herself, *him*, as she circulated at his side, pausing to speak to one couple after another, her smile so firmly fixed that her facial muscles *ached* from the strain of it all.

Rebecca, however, was in her element, and never far from Esther's side. Looking particularly radiant in a demurely styled blue gown, the younger girl appeared totally at ease with her fellow guests in a manner that was far beyond her years.

It was after one before the guests began to depart, and it was almost two when Nicolas, Kate and Rebecca took their leave.

'Thank you, it was a lovely party.' Kate's voice was quiet, the words a genuine compliment to her mother-in-law for her expended effort.

'You're welcome, my dear,' Esther returned warmly, hugging Kate's slim frame. 'We'll have lunch together next week. I imagine you'll feel a bit lost with Rebecca in boarding-school.'

In the car she sat in silence, aware that any lapse on her part in conversation was more than adequately disguised by Rebecca's excited chatter.

What a change the space of a week had made, she decided with wry resignation. Rebecca was a totally different girl, and so, Kate recognised, was she. For entirely different reasons.

Once home, she preceded Nicolas indoors, bade her sister goodnight, then made her way upstairs.

Twin lamps on the bedside pedestals lit the suite with a subdued glow, and Kate faltered to a standstill in the centre of the large room.

The bed, and everything it signified, was her downfall, Kate brooded, staring at the elegant décor with unseeing eyes. Beyond this room, she could wage any number of battles and not succumb. Yet here she became someone else—almost as if another spirit lay dormant deep within, only to emerge at a lover's touch.

Why? she agonised silently. Nicolas Carvalho was everything she hated in a man, and someone who had caused her immeasurable pain. It didn't seem feasible that she could forget such heartache to the extent that she became lost in his arms—a willing supplicant who behaved like a wanton only too eager to taste all the delights he chose to bestow.

A slight sound alerted her to Nicolas's entry into the room, and she stood still, unwilling to turn and face him.

The walk-in wardrobe door slid open, and she heard the rustle of clothing being discarded, the faint chink of a hanger replaced, the soft swish of a jacket being placed over the mahogany valet frame, followed by silence.

'Do you intend standing there all night,' Nicolas drawled, 'or am I to have the pleasure of undressing you?'

Kate didn't resist as his hands closed over her shoulders and turned her towards him. Nor did she make any attempt to struggle when he gently removed the coat and slipped it over a nearby chair.

Her eyes followed his action, lingering on the fur before returning to meet his dark inscrutable gaze.

'I don't believe you thanked me.'

'No, I didn't.' Was that her voice? It sounded impossibly husky and indistinct.

His eyes gleamed with latent mockery as he reached for the zip fastening on her gown and slid it down, managing with practised ease to slip the smooth silk bodice from her shoulders so that the gown slithered to a heap at her feet.

'So—thank me.'

He released the front clasp of her bra, and she forced herself to stand perfectly still as his gaze narrowed at the faint fading smudges incurred by his passion.

'In the age-old tradition?' It was the height of folly to indulge in such facetious word-play, but it was almost as if she was on a roller-coaster, careering towards her own destruction. 'If you'd care to state your preferred——' she paused deliberately '—titillation, I'll endeavour to oblige.'

It was impossible to tell anything from his expression, and she watched with detached fascination as he brushed the tips of his fingers down the edge of her cheekbone.

'I'm almost inclined to call your bluff,' Nicolas drawled, and her lips trembled slightly beneath his touch as he traced the outline of her mouth.

'Afraid I might have received tutorage in the art of pleasing a man during the past three years?' She was mad, *insane*, to taunt him in this manner.

'Be careful of your foolish tongue,' he warned in a voice that was velvet-encased steel and infinitely dangerous.

'How can you be sure, Nicolas?' she continued in open defiance.

'If I were uncertain, my reckless *esposa*, I would have afforded Rebecca only the most minimum assistance, and declined to become involved.'

Her eyes clouded with angry helplessness. 'The age-old double standard,' she derided. 'Wherein the estranged wife must remain pure and barren, while the estranged husband sates his sexual appetite with any number of willing nubile women.' Her voice assumed an unaccustomed bitterness. 'Don't bother attempting to deny it.' She managed a brittle smile. 'Tell me, how is Elisabeth these days?'

His eyes became dark obelisk shards, sheer prisms of ebony that speared her soul. 'Very well. She will be a fellow guest at a function we're invited to attend on Tuesday evening.'

'How nice.' Her gaze was startlingly direct. 'Naturally, you've already informed Elisabeth of our reconciliation.' She wanted to hurt him in a manner that would afford her some visible measure of revenge. 'One also hopes she is aware of your promise of fidelity.'

'Do I detect a note of warning?'

'I insist you honour that vow,' Kate declared stoically, and glimpsed the slight cynical twist at the edge of his lips.

'While you attempt the role of vamp in my bed?'

She hated the way her body began to react to his drawled query, and she shivered slightly as his gaze conducted an intimate appraisal of her slim curves, then returned to settle on her mouth for several long seconds before lifting fractionally to trap the glittering depths of her eyes.

'Perhaps you might care to offer a sample of what I can expect?'

How she'd like to retract her careless, *foolish* words, yet he'd cleverly manoeuvred her into a corner, and she was darned if she'd cry wolf.

'Why not?' Lowering her lashes, she slowly lifted her hands and removed the pins from her hair, letting the mass of confined curls tumble down her shoulders. 'What a pity you're already undressed.'

She was mad, she decided, to even contemplate taking such a path.

'Not completely,' Nicolas drawled, and she tilted her head, not quite meeting his gaze as she proffered a musing secret smile before allowing her eyes to sweep down to the sleek scrap of black silk sheathing his manhood.

'Patience, *mi esposo*,' she chided. 'Seduction is a time-consuming art.' Lifting a hand, she allowed her fingers to begin a delicate tracery of one muscled shoulder, trailing each patterned sinew of his chest, bypassing the nipple to his rib-cage, teasing a path to his navel and pausing there with tantalising uncertainty before creeping up with apparent reluctance to tangle the line of hair arrowing towards his chest.

Not content, she spread her fingers through the whorls of dark hair, pulling gently, before assuming a tentative exploration of one hardened male nipple. Fascinated, she trailed the fingers of her other hand across its twin, pretending a comparison between each aroused nub, before shifting her attention to the hard ridge of his collar-bone, the hollows at the base of his throat.

With exquisite delicacy she traced every ridge, every muscle moulding his shoulders, his arms, right down to each hand in turn, dedicating time to the pads of his fingers before lifting them to her lips and drawing each, one at a time into her mouth to savour as if it were an unknown morsel she needed to taste.

Her hands fell to his waist, then slid round to his back to caress the indentations of his spine, aware to her cost that such an action brought her impossibly close to him.

Up until now, she'd been able to convince herself she was a disembodied spectator, her actions calculated and contrived. Perhaps it was the brush of her breasts against the coarse hair of his chest, or the fact that his hands had somehow slid to her waist, but suddenly there seemed to be a slight shift in the degree of her domination.

Kate knew she should stop. Every instinct screamed out a warning message to reach up and touch her mouth to his, then withdraw, but some devilish imp prompted her to taunt him to the edge of his control.

Slowly she traced the hem of silk banding across the edge of his hips, back and forth, then she eased the tips of her fingers beneath the silk to caress the smooth skin, slowly moving towards the centre of his manhood.

Just as she reached that sensitised focal sheath she let her hands flutter down to the powerful muscles cording his masculine thighs, conducting a similar exploratory path until she felt his whole body tense in protective self-defence.

'If you don't stop *soon*, my provocative *pequeñela*,' Nicolas warned huskily, 'you'll undoubtedly receive much more than you bargained for.'

'What a shame,' Kate intoned with deceptive disappointment. 'When I've hardly begun.'

'In that case,' he drawled, 'maybe I should pander to your sense of adventure.'

The desire to shock was uppermost as she placed her palms against his chest and pushed him down on to the bed, then she gasped out loud as he pulled her down on top of him.

'Is this suitable for what you have in mind?'

It was a precarious position that made her all too aware of him and the power he could exert without the slightest effort whatsoever.

'A massage,' she indicated, and glimpsed the wicked gleam in his eyes.

'I guess it would depend what part of my anatomy you intend to massage.'

All her sense of coquetry fled, and she was helpless against the faint tide of pink that slowly coloured her cheeks.

'Had enough, Kate?' he taunted softly, catching hold of her hands and pulling her down until her mouth was poised inches above his own.

Before she had a chance to answer he edged her head lower until her lips touched his, then he kissed her with such devastating thoroughness that she became mindless, caught up in a maelstorm of sensation so acute that she was hardly aware that the last vestiges of their respective clothing had been dispensed with until he slowly untangled her arms and gently pushed her upward, shaping her body to accommodate the full thrust of his in a sexual possession that soon had her moaning his name as wave after wave of sensation swept her higher and higher towards a sensual plateau from which she never wanted to descend.

A long time afterwards he cradled her against him, and she made no protest as he gently rolled her over to lie beneath him. This time their loving held none of the former wild savagery, only a sweet, aching passion that suffused her body with exquisite pleasure as he led her towards blissful fulfilment.

It was late when Kate woke, and after a leisurely breakfast she helped Rebecca complete her packing. The headmistress had suggested Rebecca arrive mid-afternoon to ensure that there was time to settle in before dinner.

'I'll ring when I can,' Rebecca declared as she bade Kate and Nicolas farewell at the entrance to her appointed dormitory. 'And I'll write mid-week and tell you all about classes, the teachers, and the other students.' In a spontaneous gesture she stood on her toes and bestowed a quick kiss to Nicolas's cheek. 'Thanks for everything.' Turning towards her sister, she enveloped her in a bear-like hug, and there was a suspicious glimmer of tears evident as she slowly moved back a pace. 'Take care. Both of you.'

'You have a free Sunday in a month,' Nicolas informed her with a smile. 'We'll arrange a day out.'

'You're the best,' Rebecca responded, then, summoning a brilliant grin, she turned away and began making her way towards the broad staircase that led to her room.

'Sentiments her sister fails to share,' Nicolas drawled as he walked at Kate's side to the adjacent car park.

'Rebecca has every reason to express her gratitude,' Kate said stiffly.

He unlocked the Bentley and held open the passenger door. 'Get in, Kate,' he intoned drily. 'We'll drive up to the north coast for dinner.'

'In an effort to effect a partial truce?' she queried as she slid into the front seat, and saw his faintly mocking smile.

'We can try.'

She watched as he moved round to slip in behind the wheel, and she was unable to prevent the prickle of awareness evident as he eased the car out on to the tree-lined street.

Would they ever achieve a semblance of normality within this loveless marriage of theirs? Sadly, she had to concede it was highly unlikely.

The restaurant was charming, situated close to the sea in a small township that seemed far removed from the huge, sprawling city more than a hundred kilometres south.

The food was superb, and for the space of a few hours they managed to converse without arguing or experiencing a difference of opinion.

It was exactly what she'd needed, Kate decided, grateful that they hadn't driven straight home after leaving Rebecca, and she simply leaned back against the head-rest and closed her eyes as the Bentley purred smoothly through the darkness of the night beneath Nicolas's competent hands.

On reaching Nicolas's elegant Vaucluse mansion, she preceded him indoors, then moved quickly upstairs to undress and slip into bed, where she fell asleep within minutes of her head's touching the pillow.

CHAPTER SEVEN

KATE applied her make-up with care, then viewed her solemn features with critical detachment. It was amazing what calculated skill and cosmetics could achieve, she decided, unable to prevent the slight feeling that the reflected sophisticated image was not her own.

Her hair was confined into a contrived pleat, with a few tendrils teased free to negate the severity of style, and with a faint grimace she moved towards the large walk-in wardrobe. Extracting her chosen outfit, she stepped into the long cyclamen-coloured taffeta skirt, slid the zip fastener in place, and donned the black satin bustier with black chiffon rosettes lining the bustline. The overall look was one of sophisticated simplicity.

Expensive simplicity, Kate attested with a wry grimace as she vividly recalled its price-tag. A delicate choker of seed-pearls and matching ear-studs completed the outfit, and a generous application of her favourite Dior perfume provided a delicate fragrance that captured her essential essence.

With a faint sigh she slipped her feet into elegant black suede evening shoes, collected a matching evening bag, then slid her arms into the sleeves of a beautiful velvet coat.

'Enchanting,' Nicolas drawled with approval, and she turned to face him with a brilliant smile.

He stood indolently at ease, attired in a black evening suit, which emphasised the steel-muscled strength of his indecently broad shoulders.

Her pulse tripped its beat and leapt into quickened life at the sight of him, and with a concentrated effort she forced herself to meet the steadiness of those dark, enigmatic eyes.

'Why, thank you.' The mask was already in place, the adopted persona a well-rehearsed façade. Yet nothing could prevent the onset of nervous tension at being a fellow guest among the cream of Sydney's social echelon.

'Nervous?'

His ability to successfully read her mind was slightly unsettling, and her eyes became faintly shadowed as she opted for total honesty. 'Who wouldn't be?' she countered, tilting her head as she met his narrowed gaze. 'Everyone will imagine I've returned to Sydney in a bid to get my hands on your money.'

'Not my body?'

He was impossible. Yet there was a light bantering quality apparent, a latent gleam of humour in those dark eyes, as he deliberately sought to tease.

Her eyes cleared and assumed a defiant sparkle. 'Oh, that too, Nicolas,' Kate owned with unaccustomed mockery. 'I doubt your reputation with the opposite sex has waned in the past three years. Women flock towards you like bees gathering round a honey-pot.'

'But not you.'

She viewed him carefully, noting the indomitable façade, the faint air of world-weary wariness apparent that could only be attributed to a man well-versed in humanity and the pressures of heading a large financial corporation. She had experienced his kindness and compassion, yet at the same time she had always been aware of his ruthless implacability.

'You're a very attractive man,' she accorded with innate honesty. 'A man most women would find impossible to ignore.'

For several long seconds he just looked at her, his gaze impossibly dark and therefore difficult to read.

'Could that by any chance amount to an admission of sorts?'

An ache manifested itself deep inside her stomach, accelerating until it became a physical pain, and she swallowed compulsively, unable at that precise moment to find any suitable words with which to respond.

'I'm a prisoner in a gilded cage.'

'There are no locked doors, Kate.'

He was so close that she could smell the faint muskiness of his aftershave and sense the warmth of his skin. A potent combination that proved electrifyingly magnetic and totally destructive to her peace of mind.

'There's no need, is there? You've successfully clipped my wings.'

'Is freedom so important?'

It was crazy, but she felt incredibly sad. 'I tried it once.'

'Were you happy?'

I ached every night, wanting, *needing* you, she wanted to cry. There wasn't an hour when I didn't recall your image. And yet I *hated* you for teaching

me how to love you, for carelessly destroying my
fragile emotions.

'Yes. I grew up,' Kate said simply.

Nicolas smiled, and, although she searched his
features for any trace of cynicism, there appeared
to be none in evidence.

'Is that sophisticated hair-style meant to
exemplify the emergence of the new Kate
Carvalho?'

She stood perfectly still as his fingers brushed
the tendrils trailing close to one ear. 'The hair-
dresser spent an hour achieving this contrived pleat.'

His fingers slid down to cup her jaw. 'I much
prefer it loose in a glorious disarray of blonde curls
cascading halfway down your back,' Nicolas
drawled softly, holding her eyes captive with his,
and at that moment she felt ill-equipped to deal
with his degree of blatant sensuality.

'You're swamping me,' Kate reiterated quietly,
conscious of every breath she took.

'Does it frighten you?'

'Yes.' Her gaze didn't falter. 'You possess an
alarming sense of purpose, which undoubtedly
works in the business arena. However, I should
warn that I'm not an inanimate possession you can
admire and add to your collection.'

'My dear Kate, *inanimate* is the last description
I'd choose to accord you.'

A vivid memory of the wanton she became in his
arms brought a soft tinge of colour to her cheeks.
It took tremendous effort to drag her gaze away,
but she managed, and her voice was vaguely stilted
as she queried, 'Shouldn't we be leaving?'

His husky laughter merely heightened her colour, and she walked from the room, uncaring whether he followed or not.

The evening was a replay of many Kate had attended in the past, the charity prestigious and attracting the city's social élite. Guests utilised the event to dress in their finest, with several of the women present displaying a veritable fortune in jewellery, while the men resembled clones in their dark formal dinner suits, white linen shirts and black bow-ties.

There were several guests present whom Kate had met on previous occasions, and she bore their seemingly gracious attempts at conversation with dignity and ease, only too aware of the swift undercurrent of supposition vying with inherent curiosity.

It was a considerable relief to discover Esther and Rafael at the same table, although something of a disturbing surprise to glimpse Elisabeth Alderton seated near by.

Disturbing, because Kate doubted her own ability to compete with the tall dark-haired beauty whose flawless figure was surpassed only by the perfection of her classical features. In her early thirties, Elisabeth was Australian-born of Spanish parents. A former model, she had married into the English nobility, managing to persuade her husband to move his business base to Australia.

Kate felt the familiar sting of pain begin in the region of her stomach, and she had to consciously concentrate on Esther's conversation, while her mind betrayed her by whirling with a dozen queries she knew she could not ask, such as . . . Is Elisabeth divorced, and, if so, is she *with* anyone?

'Kate, are you not feeling well? You've hardly touched a thing on your plate,' Esther's quiet voice intruded, and Kate summoned a smile.

'I'm fine. Just not very hungry.' She'd managed the starter, picked at the vegetables from the main course, and left her bread roll intact.

'Some more wine? It'll help your appetite.'

The half-glass she'd sipped was already having an effect on her equilibrium, and she shook her head in silent negation, choosing instead to refill her water glass from the chilled pitcher close by.

As with most charity functions, there was the inevitable collection of speeches detailing successes of past fund-raising events, a laudatory spiel for the existing president, followed by a prospective date for an upcoming soirée.

It was then the music began, and guests from various tables sought to mix and mingle as women joined together, and men assembled themselves into small groups on the pretext of discussing business.

'Would you care to dance?'

Kate cast Nicolas a momentarily startled gaze, unsure at that precise moment whether she should subject herself to being held close in his arms, or continue attempting to conjure up small talk with her immediate table companions now that Esther and Rafael were slowly circling the floor.

'Thank you.'

Nicolas issued a polite excuse to those remaining seated at the table, then led her on to the floor.

His hold was conventional, yet she was all too aware that if she dared attempt to put some distance between them the arm at her waist would tighten measurably.

The heels of her evening shoes were high, much higher than she'd worn for a long time, and she felt impossibly fragile, like a young child learning to dance all over again. Inevitably she missed a step, and he immediately drew her close in against him.

'I'm sorry,' she said at once. 'It's ages since I've been on a dance-floor.'

'Just relax,' Nicolas bade quietly. 'Like all long-dormant skills, the ability soon returns with practice.'

Like making love? Except it wasn't *love*. Merely a mutual enjoyment of sex and physical lust.

A faint shiver feathered its way down the length of her spine. They'd been together for over a week, and as yet she hadn't consulted a physician for any form of birth control. *Why* hadn't she? she agonised silently. If she became pregnant she'd be irretrievably bound to her husband through their child, unable to escape without the infant and aware that Nicolas would never allow her to leave with it.

Did she *want* to be tied to him? It was too soon to know, she thought with despair. Last week she would have uttered a categorical *no*. Now she wasn't so sure.

Was *love* so important? she queried in silent anguish, at war with her own emotions. Perhaps she should be content with a mutually convenient marriage built on trust, respect and affection.

Yet deep down she knew she wanted it all, and for all the right reasons.

'The music has stopped.'

For a moment she felt totally disorientated, and she lifted her head, her eyes naked and incredibly vulnerable for one timeless second, then her lashes swept down, shielding her expression, and she offered a slight apologetic smile. 'So it has.'

'I'm almost afraid to ask where you were,' Nicolas taunted softly as he bent his head low over hers, and she sensed rather than saw his faint smile an instant before his lips brushed her temple.

'Wondering how Rebecca is faring,' Kate invented quickly, and felt his hand at her waist tighten fractionally.

'You're hopeless at fabrication, Kate,' he mocked with amusement. 'Never mind, you can tell me when we get home.'

'I'll probably fall asleep as soon as my head touches the pillow,' she managed sweetly as he began leading her back to their table.

She almost faltered as she saw Elisabeth a few feet distant, and her heart sank as she realised there was no way to avoid a confrontation.

The tall, impeccably dressed brunette looked as beautiful as ever, and a tiny voice taunted, This is it. Face to face with her husband's former lover.

Three years ago she probably would have resorted to restrained histrionics. Now she assembled a modicum of innate good manners and forced her features to portray what she hoped was a polite smile.

'Elisabeth.'

'Kate. Nicolas. How nice to see you.'

Serene, gracious, and apparently genuine. Kate could only applaud Elisabeth's acting ability, and attempt to cull some of it by example.

'It's been a few years since you were last in Sydney,' Elisabeth pursued quietly. 'Two, three?'

'Three,' Kate qualified, electrifyingly aware of Nicolas's close proximity and his arm at her waist.

'I managed to persuade Kate to return.'

An extension of the truth, depending on one's interpretation, she thought irrationally.

'I'm glad.'

Polite, empty words, Kate decided, unwilling to comment.

'If you'll excuse us?' Nicolas began to draw Kate away, and she proffered a few token words in farewell before accompanying him back to their table.

It hadn't been so very bad, after all. Except she was shaking inside, and once they were seated she reached for her glass, holding it between both hands as she forced herself to sip the remaining contents. When it was empty she replaced it on the table, only to catch its base on the edge of a plate, causing it to topple on to the cloth.

There was nothing to spill, but the action incurred Nicolas's narrowed gaze, and she sat very straight as she pretended interest in the variety of guests present.

'Do you want to leave?'

'No,' she refused, proffering him a calm smile. 'At least, not yet.'

'My dear Kate, you look pale and incredibly fragile.' His steady gaze wreaked havoc with her senses, and it took considerable effort not to wrench her eyes away.

'What do you expect? The past week hasn't exactly been average run-of-the-mill.'

'A combination of emotional anguish and insufficient sleep,' Nicolas qualified in a deceptively mild voice, and her eyes deepened into huge sapphire pools that mirrored a degree of hurt at the faint tinge of mockery evident.

'You've really outdone yourself by being exceptionally attentive. Elisabeth,' she ventured, tilting her head and offering him a brilliant smile, 'would doubtless enjoy a verbal sparring session with you.'

'Elisabeth will manage very well alone,' he returned, and his resort to mockery was deliberate.

'I think,' Kate said with infinite care, 'I shall ask Rafael to dance with me. If you've no objection, of course?' Sweetly voiced, it carried an intentional barb that he fielded with ease.

'By all means,' he drawled. 'My father will be delighted.'

Indeed he was, and they circled the dance-floor together, chatting without any seeming constraint. Rafael was a charming man for whom she felt a genuine affection.

'Dare I ask how things are progressing between you and my son?'

'Do you want the accepted version, or the truth?' Kate queried lightly, and incurred his humorous gaze.

'The truth.'

'I could kill him.'

The laughter rumbled deep inside his chest, and emerged with muted restraint. 'Indeed?'

'He's impossible.'

'Invariably.'

'How nice, an ally.'

'Esther and I have known you since birth,' Rafael said gently, and Kate's expression sobered.

'You've both been wonderfully kind.'

'Nicolas is a complex man,' he offered quietly.

Her eyes swept up to meet his, searching for something beyond the spoken words. It would be very easy to make Rafael or Esther her confidant, to pour out all her doubts and insecurities. Yet the problems she had understanding their diabolical son required *her* solution, and any advice they offered had to be biased in Nicolas's favour, she decided sadly.

'My turn, I think,' a familiar voice drawled, and Kate cast its owner an incredibly level glance as she was handed solemnly into Nicolas's care.

The evening was winding down, and so too was the music. The lighting seemed more subdued, and there was nothing remotely conventional about the way her husband's arms drew her close in against him.

Part of her wanted to stiffen and attempt to wrench free, while a soft invasive alchemy weaved its own magic, providing an irresistible temptation to lift her arms and wind them around his neck in order to urge his head down to hers.

It was as if all her senses were stirring into vibrant life, acutely aware of the potent sensuality apparent, and the faint aroma of his aftershave emanating from the warmth of his body became a powerful aphrodisiac as it mingled with the clean, sharp smell of his clothes.

She wanted to feel the touch of his mouth on hers in a soft, evocative open-mouthed kiss, to move slowly as they were now, together, without the restriction of clothes, and to enjoy a long, lingering loving that held the promise of passion's hunger.

His lips teased her temple, his warm breath stirring the escaping tendrils of hair, and her fingers moved compulsively towards his shoulder, silently seeking his nape.

She lifted her head slowly, unaware in that unguarded moment just what was revealed in the depths of her expressive blue eyes.

'Home, I think,' Nicolas husked quietly, gently releasing her, and she walked at his side, pausing as he reached Esther and Rafael to bid them goodnight, then they were in the car, driving through the bleak, cold winter's night.

On reaching the Vaucluse mansion, she made her way indoors, then trailed slowly up the stairs to their suite, where she undressed and cleansed her face free of make-up.

Her features looked very pale, her eyes luminous and impossibly large in the reflected glass, and she viewed her image solemnly as she lifted her hands to remove the pins from her hair.

Seconds later she heard a slight sound as Nicolas entered the suite, and her fingers stilled as he came to stand behind her and completed the task before turning her round to face him.

Without a word he lowered his head to hers and kissed her, gently, and with such evocative tenderness that she simply closed her eyes and allowed herself to float into a realm of exquisite sensation.

Some time later he placed an arm beneath her knees and carried her to bed, where, after a languorous satiation that evolved into wild, sweet pleasure, she curled into the protective haven of his arms to sleep blissfully undisturbed until midmorning.

*   *   *

The next few days passed swiftly as Kate became caught up with one social event after another as Esther's guest. Together they visited an exhibition of local paintings held in a prestigious art gallery, a luncheon held to aid a charitable organisation that raised funds for crippled children, and more.

Kate held a shrewd suspicion that Esther wanted to fill her daughter-in-law's time to such an extent that she had little time to think—about anything.

Rebecca managed to put through a call on Friday evening, and Kate experienced profound relief to hear the excited enthusiasm in her sister's voice as she relayed as much detail as she could in the allocated ten minutes permitted by the school.

'How are *you*, Kate?'

'Fine,' she reassured her at once, and proceeded to give Rebecca a quick run-down on how she'd spent her week.

The days took care of themselves. It was the nights that bothered Kate, for then Nicolas swept her into his arms and all too soon reduced her protests to inconsequential insignificance as he staked his claim with a possession that inevitably left her clinging to him in wild abandon.

CHAPTER EIGHT

'DARLING, you've heard the news about Elisabeth, surely?'

Kate glanced towards the woman seated to her right, and wondered if she could possibly ignore the pointed query.

The convention-room of the inner-city hotel hosting the luncheon and fashion parade for a well-deserving charity organisation was filled with guests, stylishly attired women who dressed with an eye to being photographed and rating a mention in the society pages of the city's newspapers and fashion magazines.

Esther had produced tickets the day before, and, aware of how much pleasure it would give her mother-in-law, Kate had reluctantly agreed to attend.

Now she kept her gaze level as she schooled her expression into a enigmatic mask. Remarkably her hand remained steady as she raised her wine glass to her lips, and she sipped the contents slowly before returning the glass to the table. 'Could you be more specific?'

The superbly made-up eyes widened fractionally, and artificially luxuriant lashes fluttered with theatrical precision. 'I beg your pardon, darling?'

It had always been only a matter of time, she reflected a trifle grimly, before any one of several so-called well-meaning acquaintances considered it a duty to relay supposedly relevant information in an effort to ascertain Kate's reaction and feed the very active grapevine with new rumours.

'What precisely is it you feel I should know about Elisabeth?' she repeated with a slight smile that failed to reach her eyes.

'You *knew* she and Geoffrey divorced, of course.'

Don't so much as *blink*, Kate told herself sternly, painfully aware that she had been placed beneath a figurative microscope and her every visible reaction was minutely scrutinised. Understanding body language was an art form, and she had little doubt her antagonist was avid for an outward sign of any discomfort.

'Elisabeth appears to be coping well,' Kate managed with every evidence of genuine sympathy, and saw the other woman's eyes narrow faintly.

The conversation was rapidly assuming the proportion of a farce, Kate decided, aware of an inner determination not to allow herself to be diminished in any way.

'Well, naturally, darling. After all, it's been two years since the decree absolute.'

Kate felt the blood freeze in her veins. Two *years*. If that was true, and she had no reason to doubt it, *why* hadn't Nicolas instigated divorce proceedings so that he too could be free?

Silence was the best form of defence, and her choice to deliberately refrain from any comment brought a speculative gleam to her companion's eyes.

'Poor Elisabeth,' the woman continued, and Kate had a mental vision of her sharpening her claws for the figurative kill. Her smile widened, displaying perfect white capped teeth. 'For a while I thought she and Nicolas might——' She paused delicately, her eyes shrewdly perceptive. 'But then, here you are, back in Sydney and apparently happily reconciled.' There was an effective silence as she left Kate teetering on the edge of an imaginary cliff. 'Opportune timing, darling.'

Slay her, a tiny imp prompted. 'Nicolas can be extremely——' Kate forced a sweet smile to her lips and deliberately assumed a soft, dreamy expression as she shifted her gaze to somewhere in space beyond the woman's right shoulder '—persuasive.' It was so close to the truth, with a few omissions, that she had no qualms whatsoever in allowing this social piranha to arrive at her own conclusions.

'One concludes a second honeymoon is on the cards?'

Kate's lips curved gently as her hands fluttered with seeming helplessness. 'Nicolas invariably chooses to surprise me.'

'Congratulations, sweetie,' the other woman purred, her eyes narrowing faintly as she subjected Kate to a speculative appraisal. 'Three years has made quite a difference.'

'Thank you,' she acknowledged gravely, aware that the tiny imp effected a delighted dance of victory. Life was something of an obstacle course, she mused idly. You cleared one hurdle, only to travel a distance to be faced with yet another. The challenge was to attempt to traverse them all.

It seemed timely that the background music slowly reached a crescendo with a dramatic drumroll, signalling the emergence on stage of the charity co-ordinator, who introduced herself, then called upon the fashion presenter to announce the models and detail the various designs.

Kate assumed a calculated interest in the clothes displayed, and even managed to maintain a genuinely appreciative *divertissement* with Esther, while holding at bay numerous conflicting images attempting to vie for supremacy, not the least of which was her devastating husband.

Attempting to apply logic to his actions was beyond her, for it seemed impossible to fathom *why* he'd chosen to remain married when Elisabeth had so obviously sought her own freedom. None of it made any sense.

It was a relief when the fashion parade drew to a close, and Kate made no attempt to linger when Esther asked if she was ready to leave.

With a gracious smile fixed firmly in place, she walked at her mother-in-law's side, pausing every few steps as Esther bade yet another friend goodbye.

At last they emerged from the hotel, and Kate drew in a deep breath of fresh air, immeasurably glad that the afternoon had drawn to a close. Sebastian, who had dutifully delivered them four hours previously, was waiting with the Bentley, and she followed Esther into the rear seat.

'Did you enjoy yourself, Kate?'

What a loaded question! If she was totally honest she'd have to say *no*. Yet the event itself had been very well orchestrated, the food and wine superb. 'Yes, very much so,' she answered with a warm smile, unwilling to spoil Esther's pleasure in any way.

The car, beneath Sebastian's competent hands, sped smoothly towards Vaucluse, drawing to a halt beneath the portico of Esther's and Rafael's elegant mansion in what seemed a very short space of time.

'Come in and share coffee with me.'

'I'd love to,' Kate began with genuine regret. 'Except it's Mary's day off, and I've decided to surprise Nicolas by cooking dinner tonight.'

Esther reached out and caught hold of her daughter-in-law's hand. 'I'm so pleased everything is working out so well for the two of you,' she said gently, and, leaning forward, she pressed an affectionate kiss to the younger woman's cheek, and Kate glimpsed a suspicious well of tears misting her eyes an instant before Esther slipped out from the car.

Minutes later the Bentley entered Nicolas's driveway, and, once indoors, Kate quickly discarded high-heeled shoes and shed her formal suit, opting to change into a pale blue tracksuit and jogging shoes. Removing the pins from her hair, she twisted its length into a single thick plait, then cleansed her face free of make-up.

Downstairs, she made her way to the kitchen, where she prepared vegetables, sliced chicken fillets, and set them aside in the refrigerator. Retrieving the wok, she placed it on the ceramic heating element in readiness, then caught up a set of keys and made her way out of the house.

The temperatures were sharp and cool as a strong breeze swept in from the sea, rustling leaf-laden tree branches and permeating the air with the threat of rain.

A brisk walk would clear the cobwebs, Kate decided as she reached the footpath, aware that the exercise would do her good. Besides, she desperately needed solitude in which to sort out her thoughts.

Southern winters tended to be long, cold, windy and wet, and Sydney was no exception, she grimaced as she broke into a jog. To the north, Queensland, with its soft, balmy temperatures and long hours of sunshine, seemed far distant in every possible way.

Such a train of thought brought forth an image of Antonio, and she pondered the elderly man's complicity during the past three years. His affection had appeared so genuine that she couldn't conceive its being a façade.

She remembered the meals they'd shared together, the kindness he'd showered on her—the packs of meat from sides of beef he vowed he was unable to fit into his freezer; chickens plucked and cleaned—one for her because it was just as easy for him to kill two as one; fruit from his trees; the loan of his car when hers broke down; a mechanic who magically appeared to fix it and charged only for parts because he was Antonio's friend.

Now Kate could only wonder if Nicolas was behind Antonio's benevolence. Somehow there seemed too many ifs for her to unravel without serious answers to numerous questions, she reflected soberly, and she wasn't sure she was ready to face those answers yet.

Deep within lay a long-dormant anger that was now being fanned into renewed life as she was once more flung into the social scene that was such an integral part of Nicolas's lifestyle. While one part of her accepted its necessity, the other part resented the resultant exposure to hateful gossip.

A cool droplet plopped on to her nose, followed almost immediately by another, and within seconds the skies delivered a deluge of rain that soon soaked through her clothes.

There was nothing she could do except run, Kate decided, for there was no telephone booth anywhere on her chosen route, and away from the main New South Head Road it was most unlikely she would sight a cruising taxi.

The rain, of course, failed to abate. If anything, it seemed to fall heavier and faster, and consequently by the time she reached the gates guarding Nicolas's home her clothes and her jogging shoes were a sodden mass.

Two things happened simultaneously—the sound of a car engine and the opening of the gates.

Kate hardly needed any intuition to determine just *whose* car had fortuitously arrived, or the identity of the driver.

'*Por Dios*!' Nicolas's voice sounded explosively harsh in her ears seconds after he flung open the passenger door. 'What in the name of heaven——? Get in!'

'No, I'm too wet. I'll run up to the house.'

'Get in, Kate. Or, so help me, I'll drag you inside the car myself.'

She was too wet and cold to ignore his implicit threat, and she slid inside to sit on the very edge of the seat. 'I'll ruin the upholstery.'

'It will dry,' he said tersely, his anger barely contained as he drove the car to the main entrance.

'Go upstairs and run a hot bath,' he instructed as he slid out and opened the front door. 'And don't argue,' he cautioned with deadly softness. 'My temper is on a very short leash.'

Without a word, she pulled off her shoes, then made for the utility-room, where she removed the sodden tracksuit before slipping quickly upstairs to their suite.

Plunging the plug into the spa, she turned on both taps, then she stripped and entered the shower in order to deal with her hair.

Minutes later the *en suite* was a mass of hot steam, and after rinsing the shampoo from her hair she wound a towel round her head and stepped into the spa to soak in the blissfully hot, perfumed depths.

The sound of the door's opening alerted her attention to Nicolas's presence, and she held his narrowed gaze with undisguised defiance as he moved further into the room.

'I'd like an explanation,' he began grimly, and all her defences rose to the fore.

'It's simple,' Kate revealed with a touch of defiance. 'I went for a run. It rained. I got wet. End of story.'

His features appeared to be carved from granite, and in a controlled gesture he thrust both hands into his trouser pockets. 'Naturally, you didn't notice rain was imminent.'

'No, dammit, I didn't! I *like* getting soaked to the skin!'

His eyes flared, then became hard and obdurate. 'I'm sorely tempted to shake you to within an inch of your life.'

'I participated in a war of words over lunch. I don't need another. At least, not in the same day.'

Without thinking she picked up the nearest object to hand and threw it at him, watching with detached fascination as he neatly fielded it and carefully set it down on the nearby vanity top. His movements were deliberate and she felt suddenly afraid as he advanced to stand within touching distance.

'Enlighten me.'

'You could have brought me up to date before tossing me to the wolves!' she threw with barely contained fury. 'At least then I would have been prepared when the wife of one of your so-called friends chose to advise me Elisabeth has been divorced for two years. She then charmingly proceeded to echo my own thoughts by querying why *you* hadn't chosen to follow suit, only to conclude by according my recent arrival in Sydney as *timely*.' Her eyes flashed blue fire as her anger threatened to erupt. 'Damn you, Nicolas. Damn you to *hell*.'

He looked at her for several long seconds, his sculptured features frighteningly hard. 'Surely you've learned the most successful way of dealing with gossip is to ignore it?'

'How can I, when everyone else considers Nicolas Carvalho's reconciliation with his wife to be the hottest source of speculation among the social set?'

'In a few weeks it will be old news.'

'Meantime, I have to run the gauntlet of it all, and maintain a sweet disposition in public,' Kate retorted, her eyes sparkling with ill-concealed anger. 'I hate you for placing me in such an invidious position.' She drew a deep breath and glared at him.

'Tell me, why didn't you instigate divorce proceedings and marry Elisabeth?'

'Did it never occur to you that I might not have wanted to?'

Kate was too incensed to rationalise, and without thought she burst into angry speech. 'I guess a wife tucked several thousand kilometres away can prove very convenient, allowing you to dally with any number of willing women while providing an excellent reason not to become too involved.'

He looked, she decided, as if he'd like to beat her, and she experienced a momentary qualm at treading such a dangerous path.

The eyes so far above her own became hard and implacable. 'Three years hasn't curtailed your overly fertile imagination.'

'Your involvement with Elisabeth wasn't a figment of my imagination!'

'Elisabeth is a valued friend.'

'And I should play the part of an understanding wife, fervently grateful for what little attention you care to bestow?'

His eyes hardened fractionally, then his mouth curved to form a mocking smile. 'Are you complaining that I don't pay you sufficient attention, Kate?'

'I was speaking hypothetically!'

'Of course. You don't possess a jealous bone in your body.'

'*No.*'

'Yet you protest, with voluble frequency.'

'What did you expect? A meek little companion who'd conveniently become blind, deaf and mute simply for the pleasure of being Mrs Nicolas Carvalho?'

His mouth assumed a vague cruelty that made her want to retract every foolish word. 'Do you particularly want to continue with this argument?'

'*Yes*,' Kate declared irrationally. 'I'd like to fight you and *win*.'

His lips moved to form a twisted smile. 'Impossible. I make it a practice never to lose.'

She looked at him with stormy eyes, ready to do battle, given the slightest opportunity. 'Will you get out of here? I'd like some privacy!'

'I'll be in the study for an hour. Then we'll go out to dinner.'

'I've had enough socialising for one day. Besides, I've already prepared a meal.'

'Indeed?'

That sardonically drawled query was the living end, and without conscious thought she scooped up a handful of water and pitched it at his chest, deriving immense satisfaction from the appearance of a large drenched patch on his pristine white shirt.

Without a word he caught hold of her shoulders and hauled her to her feet, his arms enfolding her against him as he lowered his head to hers.

The hard, relentless pressure was almost a violation as his mouth forced open her own, and his tongue became a plundering force as he brought about her subjugation in a manner that had her silently begging him to desist.

Hard fingers slid beneath the towel covering her hair, and she moaned an entreaty as her jaw, her neck muscles stretched with painful intensity.

Just as she thought she could stand it no more the relentless pressure eased, and a choked sob rose in her throat, unable to find voice as his tongue continued to fill her mouth, and she clenched her hands into fists, flailing them uselessly against his back in an effort to be free of him.

When he released her she stood mesmerised for several long seconds as he slowly unbuttoned his shirt and discarded it before releasing the zip on his trousers, only to become galvanised into action when he reached for the band of his hipster briefs.

Stepping out from the spa, she grabbed hold of a towel and wound it quickly round her slim curves. A gesture that resulted in a mocking slant of one eyebrow as he activated the taps in the shower and stepped calmly into the glass-walled cubicle.

With hasty movements she completed her toilette, then moved into the bedroom to dress, choosing to don jeans and a loose knitted jumper patterned in a variety of bright-coloured hues.

As Nicolas emerged into the room Kate slipped quickly into the *en suite* and tended to her hair with a hair-drier, choosing to confine its length in a single thick braid that reached halfway down her back.

Three-quarters of an hour later the table was set and the chicken stir-fry and rice she'd prepared was ready. Activating the intercom system, she alerted Nicolas, then carried the serving dishes into the informal dining-room.

There had been a tureen of thick minestrone in the refrigerator, which she'd decided to serve as a starter, and dessert was a delicious apple crumble Mary had prepared the day before.

'Cat got hold of your tongue, Kate?'

She drew in her breath and held it for a few seconds at the sound of that slightly mocking drawl, then released it slowly as she spared him a long, considering look. 'I'm trying my best to maintain a degree of civility,' she declared with the utmost politeness, and saw his eyes gleam with latent humour.

'A difficult task, I presume.'

'Yes.'

'This is an excellent meal,' he complimented her, and she inclined her head in silent acknowledgement.

'I like to cook.' It was nothing less than the truth, and so keen was her interest that she'd studied Italian cuisine in an effort to provide Antonio with a variety of his favourite dishes.

'Antonio was quite fulsome with praise for your culinary achievements.'

Her eyes widened measurably, then became shuttered as she concentrated on her plate. 'He was a very generous man,' she said quietly, aware of the sharp edge of hurt still evident that the friendship she'd shared with the elderly Italian was little more than a shell.

'Why don't you ring him?'

'To say what, Nicolas?' she countered. 'Thanks for playing detective during the past three years?' Her eyes began to ache and she blinked to ease the pain. 'I didn't even get to say goodbye. You took control of that, as well as everything else.'

'He cares for you very much,' Nicolas declared.

Something in his tone aroused her curiosity. 'You've spoken to him since I left?'

'Of course. Antonio is a valued friend. I gave my word I'd keep him informed about you, and Rebecca.'

'Such concern for my welfare,' she said with a tinge of bitterness.

'Would you have preferred it otherwise?'

A week ago she would have rushed into angry speech. Now she hesitated, aware of the constant war she waged with her emotions as she strived to resolve an inner conflict. There were increasing occasions when she was forced to examine the reasons why she'd left Nicolas; unwilling to recognise the possibility that she'd been too immature to separate fact from fallacy, and too hurt to accept she could be wrong.

'Dessert, Nicolas?' Kate prompted, deliberately not rising to the bait.

'Thank you. After which I have to make a few international calls.'

'While I attend to simple domestic chores, watch television, then retire.' She hadn't meant to sound cynical, but the words seemed to have a dry edge.

'You want my help with the dishes?'

'I wouldn't dare suggest you venture into such a realm of domesticity.'

'I flatted for several years while attending university,' he drawled cynically. 'Like everyone else, I cooked, cleaned, washed and ironed.'

With a slightly exaggerated gesture she placed a hand to her heart and feigned unmitigated surprise. 'You did? Good heavens, I imagined you persuaded any one of several nubile young female students to take care of such chores with the promise of a restaurant dinner as a possible reward.'

'Followed by a night of passion in my bed?'

'Without doubt. All work and no play...' She trailed to a deliberate halt, her smile bright as she pushed her plate to one side, her appetite gone. 'When would you like coffee? Half an hour?' She got to her feet and began stacking plates. 'I'll bring it into the study, shall I?'

'Thank you.'

Kate missed his faintly narrowed gaze, and minutes later she suffered his assistance, stacking crockery and cutlery into the dishwasher, unwilling to say so much as a word. The instant she was alone she let out a long-drawn-out breath, then restored Mary Evans's domain to its pristine condition.

Precisely thirty minutes later she knocked on the study door, deposited his coffee on the desk, then retreated to watch television in the large, airy family-room at the rear of the house.

The events of the day had proven tiring, and several times she had to forcibly keep her eyes open as she watched flickering images on the screen, reluctant to stir herself sufficiently to switch the set off and go upstairs to bed.

It was there Nicolas found her, and he stood for a long while as she slept, his eyes vaguely pensive as he took in the soft feminine features, so vulnerable in repose. Then he gently gathered her into his arms and carried her to their suite, where he carefully eased off her outer clothes before placing her beneath the covers.

Kate was floating, caught up in a dream where Nicolas was no longer *el diablo*, and within the freedom of fantasy she moved closer, pressing her body to his in an invitation as old as time itself, silently enticing his sensual maestro's touch in a loving that was so hauntingly vivid that it became difficult to separate the dream from reality.

One day merged into another, and, although Kate genuinely enjoyed socialising, there was a definite limit to the number of functions she chose to attend.

What she needed, she determined, was something constructive with which to fill her time.

'Would you mind if I bought a sewing-machine?' she broached during dinner, and suffered Nicolas's scrutiny.

'For what specific purpose?'

'Why—*sewing*, of course.'

'Don't be facetious, little cat,' he chided indolently. 'Am I to take it the social scene is beginning to pall?'

Kate struggled with her conscience, and won. 'I adore Esther, and I admire the way she tirelessly gives so much of her time and effort to being on the committees of the various charities. Someone has to do it, and I do enjoy attending some of the functions.'

'But not all, I gather?'

'No.'

'There are a number of things you could do to occupy your time,' he drawled.

'Of course,' she agreed. 'Become a member of any one of several sports clubs, play tennis, golf, practise t'ai chi, spend a few hours each day doing aerobics. I can also,' she added sweetly, 'shop till I drop.' Her smile widened with deliberate guile. 'One of the advantages of having an extremely wealthy husband.'

His eyes gleamed with latent humour, and he took time to swallow a measure of wine from his glass before querying, 'What is it specifically you want to sew on this sewing-machine?'

'Will you be amused if I say dolls' clothes?' She hurried on before he had a chance to offer comment. 'It's a very specialised craft.'

'You see it as a hobby?'

'Yes,' she answered honestly, giving voice to something that had consumed her thoughts for the past week. 'I'd like to begin my own collection, and donate to charity.'

'Then go ahead, Kate.'

Her eyes sparkled with surprised appreciation. 'You agree?'

'Did you imagine I wouldn't?'

'I expected you to argue that my first priority was *you*, with a constant round of social obligations coming a close second,' she said slowly.

'Have Sebastian arrange the necessary tradesmen to install cupboards, workbenches—whatever you need.'

Her pleasure was genuine, as was her smile, and he drawled with a touch of mockery, 'One could almost believe this means more to you than anything else you've been given.'

'It does,' she assured without hesitation.

A week later the room was complete, and Kate spent most mornings ensconced at the sewing bench, cutting materials from patterns, then stitching them together.

Working like this brought the small cottage in north Queensland vividly to mind—and Antonio. Without pausing for thought, she reached for the nearest phone and punched out the requisite digits, immeasurably pleased by Antonio's delighted response and the genuine warmth of his regard as they talked for more than half an hour.

'Invite me to the christening of your first child,' Antonio bade her, and a deep, husky chuckle sounded down the line. 'For that occasion I will board a plane and venture south.'

Kate managed a restrained response, then replaced the receiver with a strangely pensive expression. Antonio's words had alerted her to a pertinent fact she'd been consciously avoiding for the past week. Something that could be attributed to a number of reasons, she brooded, unwilling just yet to face the most obvious one.

CHAPTER NINE

THE foyer was crowded with patrons enjoying a short interval before returning to the large amphitheatre to hear the world's greatest tenor perform the final section for the evening. The continuous chattering voices, combined with a wealth of cigarette and cigar smoke, made Kate feel distinctly light-headed as she stood quietly at Nicolas's side.

'Isn't he wonderful?' Esther enthused. 'His voice soars like a bird, lifting effortlessly higher and higher without loss of tone.'

'Brilliant,' Kate agreed, wanting only to sit down.

Esther's eyes sharpened fractionally. 'My dear,' she said gently, 'are you not feeling well?'

'Cigarette smoke tends to activate a slight allergy condition. I'll be fine once we leave the foyer,' she enlightened her with a slightly rueful grimace, ignoring Nicolas's faintly speculative gaze.

'We'll go inside, shall we?' Nicolas declared smoothly, curving an arm round her waist as he slowly wove a path through the milling patrons.

It was bliss to be seated, and when the curtain rose she relaxed and let the music seep right through to her bones, applauding as vigorously as everyone else when the tenor waved his handkerchief and bowed out, only to return minutes later to render a rousing encore.

Consequently it was after midnight when they deposited Esther and Rafael at their front door, and

Kate felt intensely weary as Nicolas brought the Bentley to a halt inside the garage of his home.

Her home, too, she reflected as she followed him upstairs to their suite, unwilling to give it much thought as she came to a halt at the foot of the large bed.

'Esther seems to think you're unwell,' Nicolas drawled as he came to stand beside her. 'What is it? The onset of the flu?' He caught hold of her shoulders and turned her round to face him.

'I'm tired, and I have a headache,' Kate said quietly, and saw his eyes narrow fractionally.

'The age-old excuse as a ruse to escape sex?'

Her eyes sparked with the beginnings of anger. 'You view a woman merely as a convenient vessel to appease *lust*? Have you never considered *my* needs might not be as constant as yours?' She retained too vivid a memory of the willing wanton she became in his arms for that particular query to hold much weight, and she was powerless to prevent the faint tinge of colour that crept over her cheeks as his mouth curved into a mocking smile.

'In that case, you'll no doubt welcome my absence in Melbourne, where I must attend a series of business meetings.' His eyes were dark, enigmatic, yet strangely watchful. 'I was going to suggest you accompany me, and spend the days shopping or viewing the many art galleries.'

She adored Melbourne, the wide tree-lined streets, the trams whirring along their network of steel tracks. It would have been a wonderful break away, and she was truly torn, wanting so much to go, yet unwilling to back down in any way. 'When do you leave?'

'Tomorrow. Esther suggested you should stay with her.'

'I care for Esther very much,' Kate responded with innate honesty. 'However, in this instance, I'll pass. Besides, your home is wired to the hilt with security measures, and Mary and Sebastian reside on the property. In any case,' she qualified reasonably, 'I'm no longer a child.' A faint smile curved the edges of her mouth. 'Knowing your mother, my days will be filled with one social obligation after another. I won't even have time to miss you.'

'What about the nights?'

'Wonderful,' she enthused sweetly. 'I'll have the entire bed to myself!'

'Aware that I'm not here to share it,' he concurred with mockery, adding softly, 'I trust you will sleep well.'

'I shall,' she said with conviction, knowing she lied.

'Do you need something for your headache?'

Kate opened her mouth, then closed it again. 'It's not that bad.' Turning away from him, she began to discard her clothes, and after donning her nightgown she crossed to the *en suite*, removed her make-up and unpinned her hair.

On emerging into the bedroom, she saw Nicolas comfortably settled in bed, and he snapped out the bedside lamp as she slid in beside him.

She lay still, unwilling to move as she deliberately paced her own breathing in an attempt to summon sleep. It didn't work, nor, after the space of several minutes, did any one of several relaxation techniques, and the headache she'd invented gradually insinuated itself into a throbbing reality.

Kate closed her eyes in the hope it would dissipate without the help of medication, realising as the minutes dragged by that she'd be better to admit defeat. With a silent groan she slid out of bed, caught up her robe and padded quietly downstairs to the kitchen.

Warm milk would help, and she poured some into a mug and heated it in the microwave, then carried it to a nearby table and retrieved a magazine to scan while she sipped the hot drink.

'Headache worse?'

Kate glanced up at the sound of Nicolas's voice, and met his dark, probing gaze. 'I've taken tablets.'

Attired in a black towelling robe, he looked vaguely satanical, and she watched with detached fascination as he moved to stand behind her, closing her eyes as his fingers began to massage the base of her nape, firmly kneading their way up through her hair to work magic on her scalp before settling at her temples.

It was heaven as she felt the tension drain away, and she murmured a husky, 'Thanks,' as his hands slid down to rest on her shoulders.

'Finish your milk.'

Kate obeyed him without question, then she took his outstretched hand and moved upstairs to their suite to slide beneath the covers.

Hold me, she begged silently. A faint sigh feathered its way from her lips as his mouth settled briefly on her forehead, before slipping down to bestow a soft open-mouthed kiss that was so incredibly gentle that it made her want to cry.

One hand curved round her waist, pulling her close, while the other slipped beneath the satin nightgown to settle possessively over one breast.

Then his lips left hers and brushed the top of her head, and like a contented child she simply closed her eyes and fell asleep.

Kate awoke in the morning to find an empty space beside her, and, on quickly checking the time, discovered that Nicolas was already winging his way south on a flight to Melbourne.

There was no sign of a lingering headache, and without pausing for thought she slid the covers aside and made for the *en suite* where she enjoyed a leisurely shower, then she donned fresh underwear, jeans and a loose knitted jumper and ran lightly downstairs.

After a healthy breakfast she read a newsy letter from Rebecca, duly reporting continued enthusiasm for the teachers, fellow students and informing her sister that she had the following Sunday free.

Kate missed Nicolas more than she was willing to admit, and to negate the effect of his absence she resorted to the greatest panacea of all—work. Witness of her efforts was an admirable collection of dolls' dresses, beautifully crafted and finished to the finest detail.

Sebastian was despatched to collect Nicolas from the airport, and it was almost five when the Bentley drew to a halt outside the main entrance—only minutes before Nicolas entered the lounge.

Kate felt a familiar clutch of elation at the sight of that tall, broad frame. Strong and powerful, he portrayed dynamic energy beneath an air of leashed control, and her eyes searched his features as he crossed to where she stood.

Without a word he lowered his head and kissed her with a hard possessiveness that left her gasping for breath by the time he released her.

'Miss me?'

His drawled query brought a faintly breathless laugh to her lips. 'I've been much too busy.'

He lifted a hand and raked it through his hair, then checked his watch. 'I've received a relayed message from my barrister,' he revealed. 'Rebecca's case comes before the court on Monday, and he anticipates she'll receive only the minimum fine. I've contacted Rebecca's headmistress and arranged for her to have the morning free. Now,' he said with regret, 'there is only time for a quick drink and a shower before we're due to dine with one of my business associates.'

She found it difficult to hide her disappointment. 'Must we?'

He lifted a hand to her chin, tilting it so she had little option but to meet his gaze. 'Dare I imagine you're loath to share me with a number of fellow guests?'

She looked at those strong, chiselled features, the steady dark gleaming eyes and firm mouth, and was unable to prevent the pleasurable ache that began in the pit of her stomach and steadily spiralled until it encompassed her entire body.

'Most women would revel in the opportunity to display their latest designer outfit, or most recent acquisition of jewellery given by an adoring husband,' he teased with gentle mockery, and she was totally unprepared when he leant forward and bestowed a brief hard kiss to her unsuspecting mouth.

'I've never bothered with jewellery,' Kate stated, longing to pull out of his grasp before her traitorous body succumbed to the magical spell of his.

'No.' His eyes became faintly hooded. 'Nor do you consider me an adoring husband.'

She opened her mouth, then slowly closed it again, the facetious retaliatory comment dying in her throat. 'You've given me many beautiful gifts.'

'On which you place little significance.'

She wanted to reach out and touch him, assure him that the one thing she so dearly wanted from him was beyond price in monetary terms. Yet the words failed to find voice, and to disguise the ache in her heart she effected a slight shrugging gesture. 'You're an important man, Nicolas, who maintains a high profile.' She managed a faint smile, although her eyes held a tinge of sadness. 'It's essential your wife complements that image.'

'You perceive yourself to be an extension of my so-called image?'

It was impossible to discern his mood, and she didn't even try. 'Four years ago we married for reasons of mutual convenience. Why should anything have changed?'

'Why, indeed?' he countered with an edge of mockery, although his eyes darkened measurably as he lifted a hand and brushed his fingers across her cheekbone. 'Although this time round you'd do well to be aware I won't tolerate a further separation.'

A sparkle of defiance lit her eyes, turning them into bright, clear sapphire, though she kept her voice steady. 'A wife whose payment is the occupation of her husband's bed, and the granting of sexual favours on demand. And, of course,' she added with a deliberate lack of guile, 'the acceptance that her body be utilised as an incubator for his child.' She was dying inside, but it didn't show. His eyes flared, then became hard and inflexible, and for the first time she experienced real fear.

'I'm tempted to demonstrate the many ways in which a man can *use* a woman,' he began with chilling slowness. 'Then you would weep, and wish you'd never been born. Believe me.'

It took every ounce of resolve to hold his gaze, but she managed it, even though deep within she felt as if she were slowly shattering into a thousand pieces. Don't you see *me*? she longed to cry out. Who I am, what I *feel*? Flesh and blood, with real emotions—not a reasonably attractive, personable female content merely to dance to a master's tune?

Capitulation was obviously the wisest choice, and her lashes swept down, veiling her expression. 'I'll get changed.'

Choosing what to wear hardly posed a problem, and she simply selected one of several suitable gowns in her wardrobe. The turquoise satin dress with fold-over skirt, demurely draped neckline and slim-fitting elbow-length sleeves was a perfect foil for her pale creamy skin, sapphire-blue eyes and ash-blonde hair.

She was too pale, she decided on analytical appraisal, opting to tone in more blusher and add another application of mascara. Choosing to wear her hair loose, she attached side-combs to keep it in place.

Shoes were elegant black suede with a patterned swirl of minuscule *diamantés*, and she silently slid her arms into the velvet coat Nicolas held out for her before catching up an evening bag.

Kate told herself she didn't care where they were going, or with whom they were to dine. Nicolas drove, and she sank back against the comfortable leather seat, her eyes fixed to the windscreen as they swept down the New South Head Road.

Most homes were lit, their windows veiled by a variety of coverings, and she was aware of bright street-lighting and the constant probe of oncoming headlights. The sky was a dark indigo, almost black, with only a glimpse of sprinkling stars, and every now and then the sound of an impatient car horn intruded as they neared the city.

A commuter train traversed the harbour bridge, sleekly smooth on its steel tracks, and Kate looked into the lit carriages, wondering idly about the people it carried before it swept out of sight.

The silence within the confines of the car merely heightened her nervous tension, and, although she longed to break it, there was little to offer except instigate a stilted conversation that would only sound pathetically inane.

It wasn't until the Bentley slowed, then swept into a long curving drive, that she felt the familiar clutch of nerves inside her stomach, and she subconsciously straightened her shoulders and drew in a long deep breath in an attempt to summon some semblance of calm. *Act*, a tiny voice urged. Smile, and no one will ever know you're breaking up inside.

'Franca and Manuel Ferres,' Nicolas informed her by way of introduction as the door opened to reveal their host and hostess.

The home was a visual attestation to its owners' wealth, and Kate moved easily at Nicolas's side as Franca escorted them into a large, luxuriously appointed lounge, where one entire wall comprised floor-to-ceiling plate glass with a million-dollar view of the city and harbour.

Fellow guests mingled in couples and groups, the men formally attired in dark dinner suits, while the women vied with each other for supremacy in the fashion stakes.

Kate glimpsed a few vaguely familiar faces, and graciously accepted a sharp white wine from a proffered silver tray.

Almost immediately a woman detached herself from one group and swayed elegantly towards them, her perfect figure swathed in black velvet that clung with loving care, its tight skirt finishing several inches above slender-boned knees and revealing beautifully slim legs encased in sheer black silken hose. The features were nothing less than perfection, her make-up an art form, her dark auburn hair sleekly styled away from her face and caught into a tightly coiled knot high at the back of her head.

'Nicolas, darling. You've arrived.' The voice was a practised purr, Kate noted with detached interest, aware that the woman was pure thoroughbred feline.

'Dita,' Nicolas acknowledged, and, turning slightly towards Kate, he caught hold of her hand and threaded his fingers loosely through hers. 'I'd like you to meet my wife. Kate—Dita Alveria.'

'*Kate*.' The delicate emphasis held deliberate charm that any woman with sufficient nous would regard with extreme caution. 'How nice to finally meet you.' She threw Nicolas a glance of veiled coquetry before swinging back to regard Kate with contrived ease. 'I was beginning to wonder if you really existed.'

'As you can see, I do,' Kate responded quietly, her gaze steady as she summoned a polite smile.

Dita effected a husky laugh. 'Don't hang on to him quite so tightly, darling.' Her smile widened to show perfect white teeth. 'He's quite safe.'

Kate's mouth curved into a soft, winsome smile, and her eyes widened with deliberate guile. 'Actually, he's hanging on to me.'

Nicolas's fingers tightened fractionally, and Kate carefully dug the tips of her nails into his palm in silent retaliation.

Dita's brilliant topaz eyes glittered, then assumed a calculated appraisal that was totally at variance with the curving sensuality of her practised smile. 'I believe we've been seated together at dinner.'

Oh, *joy*, Kate accorded silently. The evening promised to be even more of a charade than she had envisaged.

Worse, she decided minutes later, as none other than Elisabeth Alderton appeared in the doorway, escorted by Manuel Ferres.

If Nicolas observed Elisabeth's entry into the lounge he gave no sign, although when Kate attempted to pull her hand free his fingers tightened fractionally, preventing her escape.

Dinner seemed to last forever, with a variety of courses too numerous to mention. Fine wine flowed in abundance, although after her initial glass Kate opted for chilled water.

The very beautiful Dita was seated directly opposite with a man many years her senior who was introduced as her husband. Elisabeth was seated to his left, and Kate was unable to prevent the wild thought that both women were in a direct line to gain Nicolas's attention.

'Tell me, Kate, is Nicolas planning to set you up in business? A boutique, perhaps?'

The query came from the man seated to *her* left, whose voice was ostensibly polite while his eyes quite frankly roved her delicate features. His knee touched hers beneath the table, and Kate quickly moved hers, hoping it was accidental.

'Something to fill in a few hours here and there as an interest, while a manageress takes the responsibility?' Her eyes were clear blue and tinged with contrived humour. 'I doubt I'll have the time. Nicolas has visions of keeping me barefoot and pregnant.' Turning towards her husband, she placed the tip of her nail on his hand and ran it lightly down the length of one of his fingers. 'Three boys and a girl, I think you said, didn't you, darling?'

Nicolas's eyes gleamed with latent amusement as they met hers, then he shifted his hand slightly and captured her fingers, carrying them to his mouth to kiss each in turn with lingering ease. 'As long as one is a beautiful, assertive little girl like her mother.'

He looked, for one blazingly electric second, as if he meant every word. Then his eyes became veiled, and she summoned a brilliant smile as she pulled her hand free from him.

It was a dangerous game, and one she shouldn't be playing, but she couldn't resist one last parry. 'Really, darling,' she chided gently. 'We are among guests.'

'Who will understand if we leave early,' Nicolas drawled with a thread of indulgent amusement.

Dessert was served, and Kate looked at the elegant mousse, topped with slivers of fresh fruit, wondering how she could possibly eat it. Even the selection of cheeses with wafer-thin water biscuits failed to tempt her, and she managed to indulge in meaningless conversation with another guest, seated diagonally opposite.

Coffee and liqueurs were served in the lounge, and it was a pleasant relief to move from the table. Although several minutes later she wasn't so sure, for it seemed almost calculated that Dita's husband engaged Nicolas's attention as Dita clearly sought *hers*.

'You really must tell me,' the auburn-haired beauty purred, her claws barely sheathed, 'how you and Nicolas got back together.'

'Must I?' Kate queried, wide-eyed and innocent as she sipped the delicious coffee.

'Oh, come now, darling. Your attempt to play the adoring wife lacks a certain——' she paused, her eyes faintly pitying '—emotional depth.'

'Why not ask Nicolas?' she returned quietly. 'Anything I say will probably be disregarded or used against me.'

'Your husband is a very——' Dita came to a deliberate halt '—intriguing man.'

'Yes, isn't he?' Kate felt rather like a harmless insect beneath a microscope, and she had no intention of remaining there to see if her tormentor intended to pull off her wings. Besides, if she stayed in Dita's company a second longer she was liable to say something totally regrettable. 'Excuse me.' From the frying-pan straight into the fire, she determined seconds later as she came face to face with Elisabeth Alderton, knowing she should have clung like a limpet to Nicolas's side. Independence was a fine thing, but it took immeasurable courage, especially within this social group.

'Elisabeth,' Kate acknowledged, and, deciding that she should make the best of things, she launched into polite conversation. 'So nice to see you again.'

'Thank you.'

Her smile appeared genuine, if a trifle reserved, and Kate had the instinctive feeling that there was a lack of artifice apparent. The knowledge was something she found puzzling. Either Elisabeth was an exceptional actress, or... *What*? a tiny voice taunted.

It took very little effort to recall the gossip that had circulated during those initial few months after their marriage, coupling Elisabeth with Nicolas, or the resulting accusations she had flung at him in temper. Only once, she recalled, had he denied any involvement, and she hadn't listened, convinced that there was more truth in gossip and innuendo than any words he might offer as a salve to the contrary.

Now she began to wonder if she might have been wrong. Three years' absence from the social scene enabled her to see beyond the superficiality, almost, she thought with a touch of cynicism, as if a mythical veil had been lifted from her eyes.

'Nicolas has been a very good friend to me for a long time,' Elisabeth offered quietly. 'It means a great deal to see him happy.'

Kate wasn't sure what to say. *Was* Nicolas happy? She had to admit she'd been too caught up with her own emotions to even think of examining *his*.

'Would you consider having lunch with me?'

She heard the words, and looked momentarily startled, for an invitation was the last thing she expected. More than three years ago she would have uttered a polite refusal and turned on her heel. Now she regarded Elisabeth carefully, and decided she had nothing to lose.

'Thank you, I'd like that.'

'Tuesday of next week? I'll ring you and confirm, shall I?'

'Please do.'

The intervention of Franca, enquiring if they'd like more coffee, precluded further conversation, and Elisabeth moved away to join another group as Kate was drawn into a meaningful conversation with the man who'd sat next to her at dinner.

'Nicolas is a very fortunate man,' he complimented her, his eyes roving her visible features with overt appreciation.

'Indeed,' Nicolas drawled from behind. 'Ready, darling? I have to place a call to London at eleven.'

'You hardly needed to rescue me,' Kate declared as the car drove smoothly through the night.

'Esteban is well known for his weakness with attractive women,' Nicolas declared mildly. 'Blondes are his speciality.' He spared her a brief glance as he waited for traffic-lights to change. 'If I hadn't intervened when I did he would have taken it as an indication I had no objection to permitting you a harmless dalliance.'

'Define "dalliance".'

'A few phone calls; an assignation involving lunch.'

Kate felt the breath choke in her throat. 'You think I'd *accept* such an invitation?'

'No,' he drawled. 'I merely ensured it wasn't offered. Esteban can find someone other than my wife with whom to indulge his little games.'

'Dita——'

'Is a beautiful predator who is bored with her husband and actively intent on seeking another.'

'Such—*interesting* friends you have.'

'Acquaintances,' he elaborated drily. 'Manuel Ferres is a business associate, and tonight was merely a social occasion.'

'Providing yet another visual example of our togetherness?'

'Would you have rather I attended alone?'

Imagining how Dita Alveira would have honed in on Nicolas made her feel physically ill, and she was unable to prevent the slightly waspish tone in her voice as she resorted to sarcasm. 'At least one female there would have preferred my absence.'

'You doubt my ability to cope with such women?'

'I'm sure it's your—*abilities*,' Kate paused, giving the word delicate emphasis, 'they find irresistibly attractive.'

His husky laughter was the final straw, and she retreated into indignant silence for the remainder of the drive home.

Kate opened her door as soon as the car slid to a halt in the garage, uncaring that Nicolas followed almost immediately behind her, and once inside she made straight for the stairs, only to be brought to an abrupt halt as firm fingers closed round her upper arm and swung her round to face him.

His mouth covered hers in a searing kiss that was nothing less than a total possession, and her attempts to pull free were rendered ineffective as he drew her close in against him. When he finally lifted his head her eyes were filled with pain, and she extricated herself from his grasp only because he allowed her to do so.

'I'm going to bed.' The words sounded impossibly husky as she uttered them, and, without pausing, she turned and made her way upstairs.

On reaching their suite, Kate slipped off her coat, then dispensed with her clothes before crossing to the *en suite* to remove her make-up. Catching up a nightgown, she slid it over her head, then walked into the bedroom, only to come to a halt at the sight of the large bed.

Television or flipping the pages of any one of several magazines was infinitely preferable to *waiting* between the sheets until Nicolas joined her, and without thought she caught up a velvet robe and moved quickly from the room.

In the kitchen she decided more coffee would only keep her awake, and she filled a glass with iced water instead, carrying it through to the informal studio in the rear corner of the house. Solely an entertainment-room, it housed an arsenal of audio-visual equipment, an entire wall shelved with books, together with a variety of comfortable chairs.

Slipping down into a chair, Kate tucked her feet up beneath her, and flicked the remote-control unit to operate the television.

Half an hour later Nicolas walked into the room, and she glanced up from an enthralling documentary to meet his narrowed gaze.

'Not tired?' His drawl sent shivers down the length of her spine, and she deliberately forced herself not to look away.

'Unwilling to go to bed.'

'That's an elusive statement I'm inclined to insist you clarify.'

'Read into it anything you like,' Kate dismissed with apparent carelessness.

'A fit of the sulks?'

'No, dammit! For *weeks* I've been confronted by a bevy of beautiful women who have each implied a past liaison with you. Tonight was the last straw!'

'Refusing to go to bed with me is a form of punishment?' His silky voice held a thread of amusement that merely succeeded in making her impossibly angry. 'For me? Or you?'

'*You*, of course! I couldn't care less.'

Without a further word he crossed the room and calmly flicked off the television, then he hauled her over one shoulder and strode towards the stairs, depressing light switches along the way.

'Put me *down*.' The indignity of being carried in such a manner was galling, and she bunched her fists, flailing them against his back as he carried her steadily towards their suite.

In the bedroom he dropped her down on to the bed, removed her robe, then followed her, easily catching hold of her hands as she launched into an attack, and she was powerless to prevent his mouth closing over hers.

Expecting a further annihilation, she was unprepared for the deliberate sensuality apparent, or the soft, drugging sweetness that swept through her body like wildfire.

It was akin to drowning, and soon she became caught up in a maelstrom of emotion that threatened to tip her over the edge of sanity as his lips began a slow exploratory path over every inch of her skin, lingering over-long at several vulnerable pulse-beats before centring his attention on the utmost core of her femininity.

Silently begging, she clenched her fingers into her palms, yet she felt no pain, and she felt like a disembodied spectator, aware of the soft guttural moans emerging from her throat, yet unwilling to believe they actually belonged to *her* as she was swept high on to an elusive illusory plateau from which she never wanted to descend.

Slowly he withdrew, and she dimly heard the rustle of discarded clothing, then he pulled up the covers and slid in beside her.

As he gathered her close his lips brushed her temple. 'Couldn't care less, Kate?' he mocked softly.

She couldn't sleep. Long after she heard his slow, even breathing she was still awake, her thoughts a chaotic mess. As damning as his words were, she could no longer deny their truth. Her body was its own traitorous mistress, attuned to this man in a way that fragmented her emotions and destroyed every ounce of reason she possessed.

CHAPTER TEN

SUNDAY provided weak winter sunshine in between low, ominous clouds, which appeared mid-morning and threatened the onset of rain. After collecting Rebecca from boarding-school, Nicolas drove to his parents' home for a leisurely family lunch, then, by tacit agreement, Nicolas and Kate took a considerably subdued Rebecca to the cinema and followed it with dinner in an exclusive and intimate French restaurant.

'I just wish it were all over,' Rebecca agonised as the Bentley traversed the New South Head Road towards Vaucluse. 'I've never been in a court-room before.'

'Your case is first up in the morning,' Nicolas informed her. 'For the presiding judge it's merely one of several scheduled for the day. The court clerk will read out your offence, the barrister will present facts and ask a few questions, and the judge will apportion a fine.' He spared a quick glance via the rear-view mirror, then offered lightly, 'Kate and I will be in the court-room for moral support.'

'You really think I'll be OK?' Rebecca queried anxiously as the car drew to a halt adjacent to the main entrance of Nicolas's home.

'I'm sure of it.'

Ten minutes was all it took to dispel several weeks' anxiety, Kate discovered with relief as they left the court-room the following morning.

Rebecca's euphoria was a palpable entity as she flung her arms around first Nicolas, then Kate.

'Life is *wonderful*,' the young girl enthused as the Bentley deposited her outside the door of her house dormitory. 'Thanks to you both.'

While *my* ultimate fate still has to be resolved, Kate decided silently as Nicolas headed the car towards the city.

'An early lunch, Kate? There's an hour to spare before I must attend a meeting.'

She looked at him carefully, sensing his pre-occupation. 'An hour in which you'd prefer to liaise with your secretary,' she managed with an easy smile. 'I need a few things I can easily pick up in town. I'll find a nice café, then browse for a while.'

'Ring Sebastian when you've finished. He'll come and collect you.'

'I'll take a taxi home.'

He checked the traffic, then slid into the kerb, and she reached automatically for the door-clasp.

'Thanks for ensuring Rebecca got off as lightly as possible.'

His eyes searched hers for a long few seconds, then he smiled. 'Don't hold dinner for me, Kate. This afternoon's meeting could easily progress far into the evening.'

Slipping out from the seat, she closed the door behind her, then watched as he pulled out into the traffic and disappeared from view.

It was late when she arrived home, and she opted to have a bowl of Mary's thick minestrone for dinner, followed by a generous slice of apple pie, after which she retired upstairs to the sitting-room adjoining the master suite, where she watched television until ten, then showered and slipped into bed.

Kate slept so deeply that she wasn't aware when Nicolas arrived home, and in the morning when she woke the only evidence of his presence through the night was rumpled covers on his side of the bed and an indentation where his head had rested on the pillow.

Most of the morning was spent in a state of suspended apprehension as she prepared herself to meet Elisabeth Alderton for lunch.

Kate felt nervous—*uneasy*, she corrected silently as she entered the restaurant, checked with the hostess, then followed in her wake to a table discreetly positioned in a distant corner.

Elisabeth was already seated, and she glanced up as Kate reached the table, a smile widening her beautifully painted mouth.

'Sorry I'm late,' Kate apologised as she slipped into the seat held out for her. 'I decided to drive, and I'd forgotten what a hassle it is trying to park in the city.'

'I was held up by a phone call, and wasn't exactly on time myself,' Elisabeth relayed smoothly. 'What would you like to drink?'

'Oh, mineral water,' she said at once, placing her order with the wine steward, who had magically appeared at the table. Picking up the menu, she perused the contents, then selected prosciutto and melon as a starter, followed by a garden salad, and finished up with a fresh fruit *compote*.

It was difficult to be openly friendly with someone she believed to have had an affair with her husband, and her efforts to converse held a measure of restraint, almost stilted reserve.

As soon as the main course had been served, Elisabeth picked up her cutlery, then placed it down carefully beside her plate.

'I can see you're curious as to why I asked you to meet me.' Her smile looked faintly strained, and there was a slight wariness apparent, almost as if she expected the younger girl to stand up and leave. 'The invitation should have been extended more than three years ago. I wanted to, very much,' she assured her. 'However, Nicolas was confident the situation would resolve itself without my intervention.' She regarded Kate steadily, and there was regret evident in her voice as she continued, 'He thought you would view any reassurance that my friendship with him was entirely innocent as contrived rather than a genuine attempt at the truth. The gossip circulating at the time had reached its zenith, and you were very young. Too young not to be badly hurt by it, and, sadly, too immature to accept anything I said to the contrary.' She spread her hands in a gesture of helplessness. 'You wouldn't even accept Nicolas's reassurance.'

Kate sat immobile, unable to offer so much as a word, and she watched silently as Elisabeth lifted her glass with a slightly shaky hand and took a long swallow.

'It might help you to understand that Geoffrey and Nicolas were very close friends—the three of us were. Geoffrey's health began to suffer, and it tore him apart. He had always been so disgustingly fit, eating the right foods; he didn't smoke, and he drank very little alcohol. He was diagnosed as having a rare incurable muscular disease, and he failed to accept I could continue to care for a man who would eventually become a mere shadow of his former self.' She took a deep breath and then continued with obvious pain. 'He distanced himself completely from me, refusing my help in any way, developing irrational mood swings, which were extremely difficult for me to handle. A few months after your marriage to Nicolas things began to get worse. Geoffrey insisted on the services of a live-in nurse long before one was actually necessary, and I assumed control of the business, which, thanks to Nicolas's interest, continued to perform well.'

Elisabeth paused as the wine steward refilled her glass, and she took time to fork a few morsels of food into her mouth.

'If word had got out that Geoffrey was ill, the shares would have taken a disastrous plunge, so it was arranged to reveal the information that Geoffrey had opted to work from home. With advanced electronic technology this was entirely feasible. Occasionally Nicolas persuaded me to attend a social function, mainly to remove me from the house and the constant ongoing trauma of my husband's illness. Nicolas became my rock. Unfortunately, Nicolas's kindness was misconstrued, and, with Geoffrey failing to put in an appearance on a social level, the gossip began. Before long it had swept out of all proportion. Inevitably, it reached you.'

Kate was silent for a long time, then she offered slowly, 'Like a fool, I ran.'

'Yes.'

Seizing courage with both hands, Kate said quietly, 'The gossip has it you divorced your husband two years ago.'

Elisabeth looked as if she was having difficulty summoning the necessary words. 'Geoffrey filed for divorce. I didn't contest it.' Her chin tilted fractionally as she clearly gathered in a reserve of strength. 'Three months ago he died.'

Kate felt a wave of sympathy for the woman's obvious grief, and she reached out a hand, placing it over Elisabeth's in an impulsive gesture. 'I'm sorry.'

'Thank you.' Her smile of relief was genuine. 'Shall we both have a drink? I know I need one.'

It was almost four o'clock when Kate left the city and headed towards Vaucluse. The past few hours had been illuminating, to say the least, and, although Elisabeth's disclosures had cleared up some of Kate's doubts and insecurities, there were still a few queries to which she needed an answer.

Somehow Kate doubted that Nicolas had revealed the real reason for his marriage. Yet one of her theories, that he'd married merely to provide a smokescreen for a continuing affair with Elisabeth, now held no basis for fact.

Had Nicolas really *wanted* to marry her four years ago? And if he had—*why*? It couldn't have been for *love*—could it? *Could it*?

A car horn blasted her back to the present, and, seeing that the lights had changed, she quickly eased the car forward through the intersection.

Nicolas left the next morning for a series of business meetings in Adelaide that would encompass the best part of two days.

On this occasion he hadn't even asked if Kate would care to accompany him, and she wasn't sure whether to feel peeved or relieved at the thought of spending a couple of days alone.

Introspection was unavoidable, and she felt like a small child pulling petals off a daisy as she alternated between imagining he cared for her to being convinced he viewed their marriage merely as one of mutual convenience.

Impossibly cross with herself, she made an appointment with the doctor the following day, and accepted a luncheon date with Esther, sure that the only way she'd survive the ensuing thirty-six hours was to allow herself the minimum time in which to brood.

The confirmation of her pregnancy seemed a mere formality, and she literally *floated* out of the surgery with the knowledge that she was carrying Nicolas's child.

She felt like shouting her news to Esther, Rebecca—or at least ringing Nicolas and acquainting him with the fact that he would be a father in just under eight months' time.

Except she did neither, and planned an elaborate dinner, which she helped Mary prepare, then gave the kindly housekeeper the rest of the afternoon off.

An hour before Nicolas's expected arrival Kate showered, then dressed with care, choosing a loosely pleated long-sleeved dress in yellow silk muslin. She left her hair free of confinement, and it flowed past her shoulders in a glorious mass of curls. Make-up was understated, with a touch of blusher to her cheeks and the merest hint of shadow and mascara to accentuate her eyes.

A quick glance at her wrist-watch revealed that she had ten minutes to spare, and she made her way downstairs to the kitchen.

Everything was ready, and Kate ran a quick eye over the contents of the dishes kept warm on the heated tray; then she made her way into the dining-room.

The table was set with white damask and matching napkins, crystal flutes, fine silver and bone china, and she had fashioned the exquisite floral centrepiece from pale lilac orchids.

All day she'd been aware of a mounting anticipation, and now the butterflies in her stomach began to beat a nervous tattoo in excitement at the thought that within minutes Nicolas would be home.

Half an hour later she was still waiting, and at seven she began consciously listening for the phone, barely able to contain the terrible premonition that only an accident could have delayed him.

At seven-thirty the sudden peal of the phone sounded loud in the silence of the house, and she leapt to answer its insistent summons with a shaking hand.

'Kate.'

The sound of Nicolas's voice brought an enormous wave of relief flooding through her body, and she clutched the receiver tightly as she uttered an acknowledgement.

'I'll be delayed—half an hour, maybe longer. The flight was late in, I had to stop by the office to retrieve an updated spreadsheet, and on the way home some idiot ran a red light and hit the car. Neither Sebastian nor I are hurt and the car is driveable, but we'll be tied up for a while giving statements to the police. Incidentally, I've already eaten.'

Kate slowly replaced the receiver, and retraced her steps to the dining-room. This wasn't the way it was supposed to happen, she decided wryly as she returned all the cutlery, crystal and china to the cabinet; then she removed the centrepiece and the napkins, and folded the tablecloth.

In the kitchen, she disconnected the heating tray and transferred all the serving dishes to the refrigerator. Then she went upstairs and changed into jeans and a colourful knitted jumper.

Ten minutes later she was comfortably curled up on a chair, watching television, munching segments from a plate of freshly peeled fruit.

It was after nine when she heard the front door close, and she rose to her feet, deliberately slowing her footsteps as she crossed the room.

His frame filled the doorway, his dark business suit and crisp white shirt lending him an air of sophistication she doubted she would ever be able to come to terms with, and her eyes flew to his chiselled features, seeing the grooves slashing each cheek, and the faint brooding quality apparent. Eyes as dark as ebony captured hers, and for some reason she felt inexplicably nervous as he moved towards her.

'How are you?' The words left her lips as a polite query, and she almost groaned aloud at her own restraint.

One eyebrow lifted in a mocking slant. 'No welcome kiss?'

'Of course.' Her heart thumped, then settled into a quickened beat as she reached up to place cool lips against the edge of his mouth.

His eyes searched hers, dark and impossibly difficult to fathom. 'Not exactly what I had in mind.'

Kate wanted to wind her arms up round his neck and be enfolded close against him. Yet she couldn't quite bring herself to do it, and instead she stood hesitantly, unsure, desperately needing some excuse to move away.

'Shall I get you a drink?'

'A small measure of whisky over ice.'

It was a relief to have an excuse to do something, and she crossed to the drinks cabinet, mechanically selecting a glass, ice and whisky, then solemnly handed it to him.

'How bad is the Bentley?'

He moved his shoulders imperceptibly. 'Some damaged panel- and paint-work. Nothing major.'

Her eyes searched his, unsure whether he had deliberately made light of the accident. 'You really weren't hurt?'

'No, my sweet wife,' he drawled. 'We took a sizeable jolt, that's all. Why?' he queried with a degree of mockery. 'Would you have cried tears over my broken body in hospital?'

The colour drained from her face as she envisaged him injured and in pain, his strong limbs swathed in plaster and bandages. 'That's a terrible thing to say,' she managed in a strained voice, and she turned, needing to get away from him.

She only managed two steps when firm fingers curled round her arm as he swung her back to face him, and she didn't even have time to cry out as his mouth fastened over hers in a kiss that plundered the very depths of her soul.

It seemed an age before the pressure eased to a gentler, more seductive exploration, and when he finally lifted his head she actually swayed, fearing for one heart-stopping second that she might fall.

He released her slowly, his eyes narrowing as he glimpsed the suspicious shimmer crystallising in her beautiful blue eyes, and her lips trembled slightly as she summoned the strength of will to turn and leave the room.

'If there's nothing you need, I'll go to bed.' Her voice was quiet and controlled, yet inside she was shattering into a myriad broken pieces.

'The only thing I need, Kate, is *you*.'

His faintly cynical drawl was the living end. Her eyes blazed with anger, and colour tinged her cheeks as she tilted her head to regard him with restrained bitterness. 'Sorry, Nicolas. I don't think I could bear it. At least, not tonight.' Turning away from him, she walked from the room, incapable of uttering a further word.

Upstairs, she slowly undressed and slipped into bed, to lie staring at the ceiling for an immeasurably long time, and when Nicolas entered the room she simply closed her eyes and pretended sleep.

Except it didn't work, and seconds later she uttered a startled gasp when he reached for her, gathering her close as his lips brushed gently across her own.

'Be quiet, my sweet Kate,' he said huskily. 'Just be quiet, and *feel*.' His hands caressed the length of her spine, then one slid up to capture her nape as his mouth filled her with such incredible gentleness that she wanted to cry.

Without thought she began to respond, wanting, *needing* him as much as he appeared to need her.

The loving was one of the sweetest they'd ever shared, and she clung to him unashamedly, lost in the sheer sensation of his possession.

When it was over she lay in his arms, satiated and complete. There were so many things she wanted to say, words she needed to hear, that she couldn't find the strength to begin.

The touch of his lips tantalised her temple, their fleeting softness gently tracing a downward path to the edge of her mouth.

Tell him, an inner voice urged. Tell him now.

Tomorrow, she promised as she drifted from blissful inertia into a deep, dreamless sleep.

Kate woke later than usual to find that Nicolas had already showered, breakfasted and left for the office.

If Mary Evans wondered why the food she'd helped Kate prepare the preceding day hadn't been touched, she gave no sign, and accepted without query Kate's suggestion that she and Sebastian share it for lunch.

Tonight would be different, Kate determined as she drove towards Double Bay. Parking the car, she walked to the doctor's surgery to collect a requested copy of her pregnancy test.

A soft secretive smile curved her lips as she emerged on to the pavement, and she'd barely walked a few metres when a hand touched her arm.

'Kate. Nothing wrong, I hope?'

Dita Alveira, so elegantly attired and coiffeured, her make-up perfect, that she looked as if she were about to take the catwalk at a fashion-modelling assignment, rather than idly browsing along a leafy avenue in an up-market suburban centre.

'I'm sorry?' Kate looked faintly perplexed at the other woman's carefully contrived smile.

'You've just emerged from the doctor's surgery,' Dita elaborated with a deliberate lift of one perfectly shaped eyebrow. 'One hopes it isn't a flu virus?'

'No,' she responded politely.

An assessing gleam hardened her eyes. 'Why not take time and stop for coffee? We could chat.'

Not if she could help it! 'Excuse me, Dita. I really am in a hurry.' Her smile was bright, her voice firm, and she made to move away, only to come to a halt as Dita's fingers closed round her wrist.

'I'm giving a dinner party next week. Tell Nicolas I'll ring with the time and date. I have his number.'

'Thank you,' Kate responded gravely, looking pointedly at the fingers encircling her wrist, and with a faint laugh that was slightly off-key Dita let her hand flutter down to her side.

'I hope you're not such a fool as to think becoming pregnant will save your marriage, darling.' It was nothing less than a deliberate attempt to cause unhappiness. 'Nicolas likes his women beautifully groomed and *slim*.'

'Really?' Kate's smile widened, and her eyes assumed a dreamy, far-away gleam of bemusement. 'Since adoption is out of the question, I'll have to destroy your illusions and declare you misinformed.'

'Then you do intend having his child?'

'Eventually, yes.'

A bitter smile twisted Dita's mobile mouth. 'What can I say?'

'Nothing, Dita,' Kate returned with extreme politeness. 'Nothing at all.'

Without pausing, she stepped past Dita and made her way to her car, then drove home.

Preparations for dinner in the kitchen took most of the afternoon, then she quickly changed and took a seat at the *escritoire* in the adjoining sitting-room.

Selecting a sheet of notepaper, she completed no less than three drafts before she was satisfied with her written words, then she penned them carefully on to a pristine sheet, folded it with a copy of her pregnancy test and placed them both in an envelope.

CHAPTER ELEVEN

WITHIN five minutes Nicolas would be home. Within ten minutes he'd know. A soft, faintly pensive smile parted Kate's lips, and her eyes assumed a vivid blue sparkle. It was the most precious gift she could imagine. One given from the depths of her heart. Special.

Stepping quickly downstairs, she entered the study and placed the envelope on the tooled leather top of Nicolas's desk, then became caught in an agony of indecision. What if he didn't see it?

With an involuntary movement her fingers reached for the envelope and propped it against a star-burst crystal paperweight.

Kate opted to wait for him in the lounge, and as the seconds ticked by she became increasingly nervous.

The crunch of car tyres on the driveway was a welcome sound, and she heard the soft clunk as the car door snapped shut. Seconds later she held her breath as the front door opened, then closed.

Nicolas's actions followed a familiar pattern. On reaching the foyer, he walked the short distance to the study to check the fax machine and any messages Mary might have left on his desk. Depending on their urgency, he'd either deal with them immediately or leave them until after dinner. Then he made his way upstairs to shower and change before entering the lounge for a pre-dinner drink.

Minutes passed, and there was no sound.

A strange prickle of apprehension began in the pit of her stomach, gradually radiating until it manifested itself into sheer nervous tension.

He had to have seen the envelope, he *had* to have opened it. *Why* hadn't he come looking for her?

Ten minutes elapsed, and she could bear it no longer. Rising to her feet, she silently crossed the large room, entered the foyer, and moved towards the study.

The door was open, and she stood transfixed at the sight of Nicolas seated sideways at his desk, utter defeat portrayed by the slump of his shoulders as he gazed sightlessly out the window.

What on earth...? Her lips parted as she attempted to speak, but no words came. Without conscious thought her eyes flew to the envelope he held in both hands. An unopened envelope, she saw dazedly.

Which meant he didn't *know*.

'Nicolas?'

He didn't move for a second, then he slowly turned his head to stare at her with dark eyes ravaged by an inner torment of such magnitude that it took him a few seconds to successfully mask his expression.

'I thought you'd gone.' His voice was so deep, so incredibly bleak, that it was hardly *his* at all.

'Why?' Kate queried simply.

'You left me just such a note three years ago,' he reminded her grimly, and she lifted a hand to her hair in an unconsciously nervous gesture before letting it fall to her side.

'You haven't read it.'

His eyes hardened until they resembled polished onyx. 'I don't need to.'

'I think you do,' she said quietly, feeling a surge of unbelievable hope begin deep within. He cared. He *had* to.

'Vocalise, Kate.' His voice held wary mockery. 'It's something you're very good at.'

'Not in this instance,' she denied, watching as he leaned back in his chair to regard her with weary cynicism.

'You must know, wherever you go, I'll follow and drag you back.'

Her gaze held his with unswerving intensity for several long seconds before she voiced quietly, 'I think I deserve to know why.'

'An unexpurgated avowal?'

Kate felt as if she hardly dared breathe. 'Only if you mean it.'

'You need words, *querida*?'

'Yes,' she said after a slight hesitation. 'Yes, I really think I do.'

His eyes pierced hers, unwavering in their scrutiny. 'Without you, I merely exist,' he declared quietly. 'You're my life.'

Kate closed her eyes, then slowly opened them again, too overwhelmed at that precise moment to utter so much as a word.

'How could you doubt it?' Nicolas queried gently. 'Every time we made love it was as if I gave you my soul.'

She watched as he rose to his feet and crossed round the desk to stand within touching distance. Her pulse leapt and the blood began to course through her veins like liquid fire as a myriad sensations activated each individual nerve-ending so that she felt incredibly *alive*.

He reached out, and she took an instinctive step backwards, her eyes revealing a soft blue luminescence as she silently begged him to understand.

'Please don't touch me. Not yet. If you do,' she qualified tremulously, 'I'll never be able to finish what I have to say.'

His expression became faintly hooded, and she longed to cry out against the mask falling into place.

'Four years ago I was young,' she offered carefully. 'And too naïve to begin to comprehend what I—' she stumbled over the word *loving*, quickly substituting '—living with you involved.'

He was too sharp for her, and she glimpsed the instant watchfulness in those dark brown eyes chasing her every visible expression with the intentness of a hawk.

'Elaborate, Kate.'

Oh, lord, now she'd started there was no other course but to continue. A faint self-deprecatory smile momentarily widened her mouth, then her features assumed a solemnity that was uncontrived. 'When my mother's illness was assessed as terminal you proposed marriage as a solution, and, given the circumstances and a strong desire to please her, I accepted, sure that Esther's assurances, *yours*, were sufficient for me to slip into the persona of Kate *Carvalho* with relative ease.

'For a while,' she continued evenly, feeling as if she were about to step off a cliff into thin air, 'it was as if I was encapsulated in a wonderful romantic bubble. Then reality intervened, and the rose-tinted view I had of my life shattered beyond repair. I tried to convince myself it didn't matter.' Her eyes searched his, holding them with difficulty. 'But it did. I possessed neither the maturity nor the requisite *savoir-faire* to live a lie,' she declared sadly. 'Gossip and innuendo in vicious hands can be a terrible weapon. Had we married for all the right reasons, I would have fought back. As I was aware of the real purpose of our marriage, there didn't seem much point.'

'So you ran away.'

A funny wry little smile twisted the edges of her mouth. 'Suzanne Sloane and her two daughters had been dependent on the Carvalho family for a long time. I was determined neither Rebecca nor I would continue to be a burden.'

'Surely you knew me well enough to understand I would never be persuaded into a marriage I didn't want?'

It was time for total honesty, and she didn't hold back. 'I thought you viewed our marriage as a convenient smokescreen,' she offered quietly.

Pain etched his compelling features, and a muscle bunched at the edge of his jaw. His eyes held hers captive, daring her to look away.

'Elisabeth is a very dear friend who needed moral support through a difficult period in her life. Unfortunately, there were those of my acquaintance whose vivid imagination fed your insecurity with cruelly intended supposition. What they didn't know,' he continued quietly, 'was that I'd always admired the inherent honesty that had you fighting for independence when it would have been only too easy to accept Esther's financial help. The girl grew into a beautiful young woman whom

I came to love very deeply. For a short time I thought you loved me.' His eyes didn't leave hers for a second. 'Then it all fell apart, and you left.'

His gaze seemed to pierce her soul and lay it bare. 'Forcing you to come back, *then*, wouldn't have achieved a solitary thing. Instead, I allowed you the freedom you thought you needed, and set up a watch over you, prepared to wait until you were ready for a reconciliation. Except the twisted hand of fate intervened for a second time,' he continued gravely. 'On this occasion it was your sister's welfare, not that of your mother, that necessitated my intervention.'

'Something I deeply resented,' Kate qualified, and glimpsed his wry acknowledgement.

'Yes. You seemed to delight in defying me at every turn.'

'Together, we were a volatile combination,' she allowed with a tinge of mischief, her eyes haunting the slow upward slant of his mobile mouth.

How she longed to feel it possessing hers, deeply and with such unrestrained passion that it was almost more than she could bear not to reach out and pull his head down to hers to instigate the kiss.

Yet there was still one more thing they needed to discuss—perhaps the most important of all. Consequently, it was almost impossible to keep the sparkle from her eyes as she deliberately sought to tease him a little. 'You have yet to read my note.'

She sensed a stillness about him, a strained wariness she longed to ease. And she would, soon. But right now she held all the cards in her hand.

'Tell me, instead.'

'Open the envelope, Nicolas,' she directed him softly. 'I have a meal to serve.'

Without a further word, she turned and left the study, walking towards the spacious kitchen, where she removed heated dishes from the oven on to a trolley ready to wheel into the dining-room.

She'd almost completed the task when Nicolas entered the room, and she looked up slowly, her eyes radiating lustrous warmth and a faint teasing quality that made him catch his breath.

'Are you pleased?' The fact that he might not be had never crossed her mind, and she was rewarded with the brilliance of his gaze.

'What do you think?' he answered huskily, reaching for her, his hands sliding up over her shoulders to cup her face with such incredible gentleness that it made her want to cry. 'Are you?' His expression sobered fractionally.

The thought of a child, *his* child, growing inside her, filled her with such joy that there was no room in her heart for anything but happiness. 'How could I not be?' she queried softly. 'This baby is the ultimate gift of love. Uniquely *ours*.'

He traced the outline of her mouth, and she saw his eyes darken fractionally as she parted her lips and ran the tip of her tongue across the pads of his fingers.

Gently she took his index finger between her teeth and nibbled it tentatively before drawing it into the moist cavern of her mouth, stroking it with the edge of her tongue in a deliberately provocative gesture.

'Darling Nicolas,' she berated him softly as she slid her arms up around his neck and linked her hands together at his nape. 'I won't break if you kiss me.' A winsome smile, sweetly mysterious and infinitely evocative, teased her lips apart. 'In fact, I have something much more...' she paused deliberately, then continued '...mutually satisfying in mind.'

His eyes were darkly lambent with electrifying passion, and his teeth gleamed white as he bestowed on her a long, sweet kiss. 'Minx,' he whispered, pulling her close. 'What about dinner?'

She pretended to consider the prospect. 'Well, we could always have it as a late snack.'

His hands roved the length of her spine, one settling beneath the thick swath of hair at her nape, while the other curved over the delicate roundness of her bottom. 'I haven't showered.'

It was a delightful game they were playing with each other, and there were dancing lights in the depths of her eyes as she teased gently, 'We've only made love in the shower a few times, but it could prove to be a provocative starting point.'

Releasing her arms, she loosened his tie, then began freeing the buttons on his shirt. Dark springy hair tantalised her fingertips, and she pressed her lips to the muscled wall of his chest, then tra'' d to settle on one hardened nipple, savouring with such incredible delicateness that a gro escaped from the depths of his throat.

'What do you think you're ing?'

Her eyes lifted to his, wi and incredibly lacking in guile. 'Seducing yc . Don't you like it?'

'If you don't stop, we won't even make the shower.'

Kate gave an unabashed smile. 'The kitchen? Now there's a first.'

'And risk shocking Mary?'

'I gave her the night off.'

'Did you, indeed?'

'Perhaps,' Kate considered thoughtfully, 'you could kiss me very thoroughly *here*, then carry me to bed.'

His mouth curved with wickedly musing humour. 'First we make a brief stop in the study before we go upstairs.' He brushed her mouth with his lips, then pushed her gently away as he caught hold of her hand.

She allowed him to lead her from the room without a word, and in the study she watched as he operated a hidden switch, activating a cleverly concealed wall-safe.

Kate watched in silent fascination for several long seconds, her eyes large blue pools of incredulity as he withdrew a small velvet box, extracted its contents, then re-locked the safe.

'This is for you. With all my love.'

She didn't resist as he lifted her left hand and slipped the ring on to the appropriate finger. Much wider than her diamond-set wedding band, it had been designed as a perfect complement, with large baguette-cut stones, one after the other lining the entire band.

Kate looked at it in awed silence, then raised solemn eyes to meet his. 'It's exquisite.'

'It represents eternity,' Nicolas said gently. 'Yours and mine—together.'

She made no pretence of hiding the mist of gathering tears, or the huskiness in her voice. 'I love you.'

'The sweetest words, *querida*. Words I had begun to despair of ever hearing you utter.'

'I wanted to,' she assured him, lifting a hand to trail her fingers along his powerful jaw. 'They were in my heart.'

He kissed her, long, drugging kisses that left her breathless and aching for more, then he placed an arm beneath her knees and lifted her high against his chest.

'Where to, my beloved Kate? Upstairs?'

She was drowning, consumed by the slow tormenting pleasure of passion deep within, wanting, needing only him and the exquisite fulfilment of their lovemaking.

Then she smiled, a slow, sweet, secret smile that brought a faint bubble of laughter to her lips. This tiny living embryo nestling deep within her womb stirred her to hunger with disturbing frequency.

'Would you mind very much if we had dinner first?' She placed gentle fingers against the sensual curve of his mouth, and wrinkled her nose at him in teasing remonstrance. 'Your son,' she explained, certain that it was indeed a boy, 'seems intent on making frequent demands on my appetite.'

Nicolas laughed, a deep satisfying huskily muted chuckle that rumbled in his chest. 'Then we shall eat. And afterwards,' he promised gently, sparing her a dark, tantalising smile, 'I will make love to the little *niño's* mother with such infinite care that there will be not the smallest shred of doubt of his parents' unswerving devotion to each other.'

In the dining-room, he released her down to her feet, then helped her dish out the first course, and saw her seated before taking the chair opposite.

They ate with relaxed ease, savouring the food with genuine enjoyment, content that there was all the time in the world for the long, slow loving that would last far into the night.

For the rest of their lives—eternity.